M books

General Editor: Aidan Chambers

EAST END AT YOUR FEET

M Books is a series consisting of some of the best contemporary fiction for young people. Other books you may enjoy are:

After the First Death Robert Cormier
I am the Cheese Robert Cormier
The Bumblebee Flies Anyway Robert Cormier
The Chocolate War Robert Cormier
Nobody's Family is Going to Change Louise Fitzhugh
The Owl Service Alan Garner
The Disappearance Rosa Guy
The Friends Rosa Guy
The Outsiders S E Hinton
Tex S E Hinton
That was Then, This is Now S E Hinton
Sumitra's Story Rukshana Smith
My Darling, My Hamburger Paul Zindel
The Pigman Paul Zindel
The Pigman's Legacy Paul Zindel
The Undertaker's Gone Bananas Paul Zindel
Young Shoulders John Wain

EAST END AT YOUR FEET

Farrukh Dhondy

Macmillan Education

First published in *Topliners* 1976
Reprinted 1977, 1978, 1982 (twice), 1983, 1984, 1985, 1986 (twice)
First published in *M Books* 1988

Published by
MACMILLAN EDUCATION LTD
Houndmills, Basingstoke, Hampshire RG21 2XS
and London
Companies and representatives
throughout the world

Series cover design Ross George

Cover illustration © Hutchinson Picture Library

Printed in Hong Kong

British Library Cataloguing in Publication Data
Dhondy, Farrukh, *1944–*
East End at your feet.——(M books).
I. Title
823 [F]
ISBN 0–333–46775–2

Contents

For the pupils of
Archbishop Michael Ramsey's School

1 Dear Manju

Manju was a real Indian beauty and Bhupinder was her younger brother. Their aunts envied Manju and told her mother that she ought to use a firmer hand with her. Bhupinder, on the other hand, was a favourite and was encouraged to do what he liked. He hardly remembered their father, for the boy had been only three years old when his father died, and though Manju was older and could recall what her father was like, she didn't spend any time thinking about him. She spent much more time thinking about herself and the way she looked and about films and film stars and clothes and about the boys of Brick Lane.

'Pinder, go see where your sister is,' their mother would say and Bhupinder would have to go around the houses of Manju's friends and fetch her in. He didn't like doing it and Manju didn't like him following her around saying, 'Mummy says it's nine o'clock and come home just now with me.'

Bhupinder had been constantly told that he was Manju's guardian, that he had the responsibilities of a brother, and that good brothers didn't take these responsibilities lightly. Manju did take them lightly. She didn't seem to want to acknowledge that he was now fourteen years old and his voice was cracking and the little hairs just sprouting on his chin marked an approaching season of authority. She pinched his cheeks in front of her friends, she disgraced him by making fun of his cracking voice.

Bhupinder knew he had to be patient with her. She didn't seem to realise how much a girl's honour meant, especially in the Indian community where everybody gossiped about everybody else. He would hear the elders discuss other girls.

'She's picked up English ways,' they would say. 'She goes swimming with white boys ... no respect left for her elders ... if she was my daughter ... nobody will marry second-hand girls....'

And Bhupinder was conscious that Manju was pretty, very pretty. She had long black hair which shone like a river by moonlight, and a broad mouth and a small straight, perky nose and almond-shaped eyes and light brown skin. Her mother called her 'my fair one'.

When Manju was forced to come home, she would sit in front of the telly and grumble or sulk.

'You should become a dog catcher,' she would say to Bhupinder, 'you're always sniffing around after me.' And to their mother she would say, 'How do you think it makes me feel having this big baby trailing around after me? What will my friends think, that I can't look after myself? I wasn't eloping or something, I was only watching telly at Ritu's place.'

Her mother would look at her softly, without getting into an argument. Manju was difficult, but she was the light of her life. She was clever and she was considerate and would help their mother around the house with cooking and sewing and keeping the flat clean and reading and writing letters that had to be written, and she would even help with Bhupinder's school. She would go instead of their mother to the parents' evenings and speak to his teachers, who thought she was charming.

Bhupinder was proud of walking around with her when they went shopping, or when the community gathered at someone's house, or when they went as a family to the temple a few times a year and met other Punjabi families at religious festivals. But in their own area, or around the school it was different. The boys, the Indian boys of their locality, weren't nice. They would stare at Manju in that dirty way and pass remarks, and make him feel, if he was with her, like a weak and scared bodyguard. He knew that Manju was quite aware of the things they said, and it made him a little ashamed to know that she understood their remarks and didn't seem to mind. She liked having admiring eyes on her, looking her up and down, and she even liked their grins and the competition they seemed to have to say rude things. They would imitate the language of the movies: 'What a piece of merchandise,' and, 'The opened lotus is thirsty for rain,' in Hindi.

It was all right to say things like that about girls you didn't know, about English girls who wouldn't understand, but when it came to your own sister it wasn't to be tolerated. It was the language of show-offs and loafers, Bhupinder thought, and it made him mad. In his heart of hearts he knew that looking after his sister meant facing up to them some day. Everyone said England was a civilised country, but he knew these boys, they were uncivilised rogues and how can a man protect his family's good name with such people around?

Yet Bhupinder envied them. A few of these lads, some from the fifth and sixth form in his school, made it a habit to hang around the Nishat Café in Brick Lane.

They'd be there every day after six, having changed out of their tatty school uniforms and wearing their check jackets and flared trousers, their hair thrown back in a rolling puff like the heroes of the Hindi movies. They'd play songs on the juke box and three card flush at the tables and drink endless cups of tea, and tease the girls who passed. Some of them were Sikhs, but they didn't grow their hair and they didn't even wear turbans any more. Their families either didn't care or had lost control of them, Bhupinder thought. They were the sort of Indians who gave the community a bad name, swearing all the time, getting into trouble with teachers and the police, carrying knives and wasting their time on talk of money and sex and horse racing, singing loudly in the street as though they owned London or something. Most of the other Indian boys, Bhupinder knew kept out of the way of this gang, and yet they talked about them and their latest doings, how they bought up all the tickets at the cinema when a good movie was showing and sold them for double the price to the families who had come from all over London to see 'Bobby'; or how they had thrown six white girls into the swimming pool with all their clothes on after some argument.

One of these boys was called Manjit. He was in the sixth form at Bhupinder's school and he was the king of the Nishat pack. He had a particularly bad reputation in the area, and a worse one at school. One of his teeth had been knocked out in some long-forgotten brawl and it gave his nicotine-stained grin a look of rotting evil. Even the teachers were afraid of him because he'd do the most vile things. He was known to expose himself in the playground at school and call the younger boys over to where his gang was to have a look. One of his older brothers was in jail for stabbing a man in a fight over a woman, and Manjit boasted about it. There were gangs of white boys in school too, but they kept away from Manjit's crowd and kept to their own sorts of entertainment.

For some reason, Manjit had been made a prefect at school. The teachers always talked to him as though they were addressing someone their own age. So when Manjit and two of his tough cronies were given prefects' ties at assembly, and the Headmaster announced the arrangements for parents' day that year, Bhupinder got the uneasy feeling that the time had come.

'Our new prefects this year will help out with the Indian parents who attend the function,' the Headmaster said, and Bhupinder knew that it would mean bringing Manju to the school and facing the Nishat gang.

Bhupinder's mother received the note about parents' day and passed it on to Manju.

'You better go and have a good talk to his teachers.'

'I don't need anyone to come and talk to the teachers. I'm getting the maths prize again so you can see I'm doing all right.'

'Don't be such a baby,' Manju said, ruffling his neatly combed hair with teasing fingers, 'I won't tell them that you mutter in your sleep and Mummy wants them to know that we have to chase you all round the house with a cake of soap before you'll have a bath.'

'She's only three years older than me,' Bhupinder protested.

'She's passed all her jeezees,' his mother said. She couldn't pronounce the English letters too well. She earned her living by taking in stitching from the firm that brought pre-cut jobs in a van once a week, and most of what went on at school was a mystery to her. 'But if you want,' she added, 'I'll come and leave Manjula behind and then all your teachers and friends will know that your mother is a villager and can't speak English.'

'I don't want her wearing all that war-paint in my school. Mr Crawley is a big Christian and he thinks girls with make-up are prostitutes.'

'Your tongue will get boils if you talk about your sister like that,' his mother said.

'Go and wash your mouth out. I don't know where you kids pick up these long words,' Manju said.

'Well, it's true,' Bhupinder said. He knew now that there was no way out of it, that he'd have to let Manju come to the school. 'If Daddy was alive he'd never have let you make a disgrace of the family by painting up like a dancing girl.'

'Tht tht,' his mother said, 'your father would have been very ashamed to see you always fighting.'

'Who's fighting?' Manju said. 'The little one is just showing us what a big man he is.'

'You'll get one in the face just now,' Bhupinder said, holding up his fist. Manju grabbed his fist in one hand and kissed it lightly and bounced back before he could take a swipe at her.

'Coming to think of it,' she said, 'I'd better tell your form teacher that Mummy's very worried about you wetting your bed when you get into a tantrum.'

'Manju, go and get a bottle of milk before the shop closes,' her mother said, and Manju, seeing that Bhupinder was really getting the needle, blew him a sarcastic kiss and with mischief skating round her face went out of the door.

On the evening of parents' day Manju wore a black salvaar and black khameez with a red border round the neck and hem. It was a tight *khameez* and, as she emerged from her room, Bhupinder suspected that she'd chosen it carefully because it showed off the curve of her hips and the firmness of her breasts. She had rouge on her cheeks and wore bright red lipstick, and she had extended the line of her eyes in an upward slant in black. She wore a *tikka*, a plastic dot in the middle of her forehead.

'Look at her, Mummy. I'm not going with her, people will think I've come to auction her.'

Their mother came out of the kitchen.

'Your sister looks very pretty. Now don't start the fuss again, go along, or I swear I'll put on Manjula's clothes and make-up and come myself and shout all over the school that my son may be clever at adding up but he doesn't respect his poor illiterate mother.'

Bhupinder knew it was no good protesting. They mustn't be late for the occasion and someone had to go. He didn't want Mr Crawley including him in the list of boys whose families didn't care about them. That was the way he put it. 'We are proud of the families in our school,' he said, 'and we are sure they are interested in their children's welfare.'

'Tell her not to talk to any strangers,' Bhupinder said, making ready to go.

'Look, next time for my birthday you can buy me a spacesuit, then nobody will be able to see me and you can be proud of being a purdah-wallah family. Really, anyone would think I'm going naked to your wretched school.'

Just as Bhupinder feared, Manjit was there at the gate of the school surrounded by three or four of his cronies. They stood leaning against the gate and guiding parents to the appropriate place in the school, the juniors to the year rooms and the seniors' parents to the hall.

'Good evening, Bhupinder,' Manjit said in a funny voice, as though he was teaching a parrot to speak. Bhupinder pretended he hadn't heard. He looked at Manju to make sure she was following his quickened pace, pointing out that they had to go round the building.

As they passed, one of Manjit's mates said in Hindi, 'That would do me for a mattress.' Bhupinder's ears turned red. Still he pretended he hadn't heard. He saw that Manju had, and that she was smiling to herself.

'If I had a mum like that it would drive me to sin, Einstein,' one of the others shouted after them, calling Bhupinder by the name they used for him in school.

'They are filthy bastards,' Bhupinder said to Manju in a hoarse voice, trying to prevent his throat from squeaking.

'Doesn't the tall one have a sister called Sheila?' Manju asked. She turned as a voice behind them said, 'Yes, but not as pretty as you.'

Manjit had followed them silently for a few metres.

'I know the way, thank you,' Bhupinder said.

'I'm being polite to your sister,' Manjit said.

'You can clear off, thanks,' Bhupinder said, not turning to look at Manjit.

'Ugly boys have pretty sisters,' Manjit said.

'I know Sheila, she's quite pretty,' Manju said, and

she smiled at Manjit. Bhupinder felt like grabbing her by the arm but he restrained himself.

'Why have you been hiding your sister, Einstein?' Manjit said as they got to the door of the hall. Bhupinder waited till they had walked safely into the hall which was filling up with parents and teachers. 'You mind your own business,' was all he could think of shouting back at Manjit.

Now he felt that the eyes of the women were on Manju. They went around and talked to the various teachers. Bhupinder collected his prize, a book by Kipling, and as they walked out he saw that Manjit and his mates were now lounging around the back of the hall talking to the Headmaster.

'So Einstein strikes again,' Manju said as they walked home. She wanted to make friends, she knew Bhupinder was nervous because of the possibility that the gang may follow them. Still, she couldn't help stealing a glance backwards to see if they were.

The next day in school, during the break, one of the Indian boys in the fifth came up to Bhupinder.

'Oi, Bhupinder, Manjit wants a word with you, you'd better come.'

'He can come here if he wants me, I'm not allowed in the sixth form area.'

All morning Bhupinder had been expecting some such approach and now he felt a claw of nervousness grip his guts.

'They're saying things behind your back,' the boy said.

'Tell Manjit to get himself stuffed,' Bhupinder said.

'I don't want to be held responsible for sending you to hospital,' the boy said.

15

'I don't care,' said Bhupinder thinking that he could never find the right reply, something smart to say, in time.

When school finished he wanted to bolt home, but he felt that the word that Manjit was looking for him had spread through the school, and he didn't want his form-mates to see him rushing.

Manjit and his gang were at the gate before him. Being sixth formers they could hop it before the bell. 'Make way for mastermind,' Manjit said. He held out a packet of cigarettes as Bhupinder passed. 'Have a fag,' he said.

'I don't smoke,' Bhupinder replied and tried to pass, but his way was gently blocked by one of the others. 'You shouldn't talk to your sister's lover like that,' someone said.

'No, look, we don't want anybody to get hurt do we?' Manjit said. 'Come on, Bhupinder my brother, tell me your sister's name.'

'What business is it of yours?' Bhupinder said, looking straight ahead of him.

'Oh nothing much, I'm collecting new names for my budgie, it's called Bhupinder and it's just had a sex operation so I want a girl's name.'

Bhupinder felt his blood speeding to his temples. He turned around. There were no teachers about and some boys had gathered at a safe distance, smelling trouble.

'Give the password and we'll let you go,' said the boy blocking his path.

Bhupinder was sure that they knew her name already. Then it struck him that they wanted him to say it: 'Manju' ... and 'Manjit' ... perfect.

'It's Raquel, isn't it?'

'No, it doesn't begin with "R".'

'Or could it sound something like Manjit? Your father must have been good at reading horoscopes.'

'Get out of my way,' Bhupinder blurted, raising his arm on to the shoulder of the boy who stood before him. The boy smiled, confident that Bhupinder was half his size; the smell of aggression came off him.

Bhupinder was close to tears and knew it; the rest of them were making filthy comments now. 'You can drive an express train through a girl who has known so many men,' one said.

Bhupinder wheeled on him and his right hand struck out at the boy's face, obeying some command from deep within him, some demon that came flying out. And in the next instant, as his hand weakly connected with the boy's head, a cold shiver came over him. Manjit grabbed his wrist. At the same time he pushed the other boy away. The tears hung just behind Bhupinder's eyes now, and he blinked them away. He held his breath to prevent it from coming out in jerks and to stop himself trembling in confusion. There was what looked like a jungle of faces around him. Manjit's firm grip on his wrist steadied him.

'I'm not scared of you,' Bhupinder said and the boys laughed as the last word strained into a squeak.

'Go your way, my friend,' Manjit said, pushing the other lads aside and taking total control. Bhupinder walked forward out of the circle of hazy faces. He felt humiliated and the fear dug into his heart and liver as though it had carved a hole in his insides.

He grabbed his books tighter under his arm and he was thinking on the way home of the karate lessons he should have taken, of the gang he should have joined. They had made a fool of him and his own reaction to them scared him. He hadn't faced up, they would all know that he had backed down. He couldn't look after himself, leave aside being his sister's guardian. When his mind turned to her, he felt that his revenge was somehow tied up with her, tied up with revenge against her for putting him in this situation. If he had no sister, or at least if she didn't throw herself into the bitchy game of attracting their filthy attention, he would never have got into this.

As he lay in bed that night a net of thoughts spread out and came together, swirling through his mind to form a plan of revenge. He couldn't reason with wild animals he thought: the only way to deal with them was to shoot their leader, he had heard that somewhere, but where could he get a revolver? His thoughts ran away with him. He saw himself facing Manjit with a loaded gun pointed at the bastard's heart and saw the look of terror and repentance on his face as Bhupinder tore off his mask and revealed himself to be the man Manjit had wronged, the man whose sister had had her honour stained. But Bhupinder would show no mercy, he'd work his awful revenge and he'd walk around the city after that with a magic circle of dread around him. He would be marked as a dangerous man, and good at maths. And then the boys in the Nishat Café, leaderless, would elect him and beg him to take charge of them.

Or maybe it wouldn't work out so smoothly. Maybe the police would get him and he'd sit in Death Row for weeks while his appeal to the Prime Minister was being heard and he'd walk, followed by his mother and Manju, to the electric chair, and she would swear never to dress like a cheap tart again.

In the morning he said nothing to Manju or to his mother. He went to school knowing that if it came to a fight, he would have to take the challenge and accept a beating. He'd point out to all those who came to watch that he was smaller than Manjit, but he wasn't afraid of him. In the corridors he saw one or two of the boys who had been at the gate with Manjit, but they passed him as if nothing had happened, as though they weren't aware of his existence.

In a sense that was reassuring; maybe they'd forgotten the whole thing. Still, some emptiness remained in Bhupinder. He knew that words would have to pass before he could get rid of the ticklish fear in his spine. His pride had taken a knocking, it had been forced so low, pushed down his throat and curled up somewhere, restlessly inside him.

Two days passed without incident. On the third, as Bhupinder was settling down to a game of chess in the lunch hour in his form room, Manjit walked in. This was unusual as the sixth formers stuck to their own part of the building and were never seen on the fourth-year floor.

'Bhupinder,' Manjit said, with what seemed to Bhupinder to be a note of regret and even respect in his voice. Bhupinder looked up from his game, blinking as though a bright light had been suddenly switched on. For an instant he thought that Manjit had come to ask his forgiveness, because somehow he knew of the mountain of venom that had piled up inside Bhupinder and in his dreams he had seen this mountain explode like a volcano and come down in dreadful lava on his head.

'Just come outside one minute, man, I want to talk to you.'

Automatically Bhupinder got up from the desk and followed Manjit to the door. As they walked out he felt the eyes of the boys on them. Manjit led him to a quiet spot in the playground.

'Listen,' Manjit said, taking the forbidden cigarette out of his pocket and lighting it, 'you have to do something for me.' His eyes were searching for feeling in Bhupinder's face. They were also telling Bhupinder that he was sorry for what had happened the other day but it wasn't his fault and he wanted the younger boy to forget it, man to man.

'I've got only fifteen pence,' said Bhupinder.

'Look, I don't want to borrow money,' Manjit said with a hurt expression. Then, making a resolve to himself to continue, he said, 'Your mother is very strict, isn't she?'

Bhupinder looked at him with amazement. 'What if she is? My father's even stricter, and he works in the foundry and he's nearly two metres tall,' Bhupinder said. He didn't know if Manjit knew he was lying.

'Look, forget it, just give this to your sister, will you?' Manjit said, pulling a pink envelope out of his pocket. His eyes were pleading.

Bhupinder didn't take the envelope.

'Look, she knows, I swear by God I'm not mucking about. Take it.'

'What does she know?' Bhupinder wondered and his curiosity fought with the sense of shame that was coming over him. He took the envelope.

'If she sends a reply, you bring it to me,' Manjit said and Bhupinder looked up from the neat handwriting on the envelope into the anxiety in the hard eyes. Surely she hadn't any dealings with this son of a bitch, he thought; she has more sense.

'You never come to the Nishat do you?' Manjit was saying.

'I have a lot of work to do. My father doesn't like me going around with loafers.'

Manjit ignored the remark. 'You could come to my house any time. I always take my friends there to eat and we go to all the movies free, I know all the cinema-wallahs. Have you seen *Pakeezah*? It's coming next week.' Manjit's tongue gave a quick lick to his lips. Bhupinder could see that he was trying to chat him up, and he felt a sort of transference of power. The king of beasts was wondering what he could say to be friendly.

Bhupinder put the pink envelope in his pocket. 'All right,' he said, 'I'll think about it.'

He no longer felt nervous. He was thinking about Manju and wondering if this fellow had really made any contact with her. He could tell his mother, he could tell his uncles when they came on Saturday and Manju would almost definitely be sent back to Jullunder, away from England, and she'd learn to behave like a decent Indian girl. 'I've got to go and take the register up for my form teacher,' he said and as he turned and walked back Manjit walked behind him as though to offer him his protection. For the first time, for those hundred paces back to the fourth-year floor, Bhupinder felt the eyes of the school on him with respect and wonder. It was not the sort of respect that winners of maths prizes get, it was more the sort that counts, that you can trade on. And yet there was something not quite right about it Bhupinder felt, something that whispered to his mind with every step that he was trading a bit of his self-respect for his feeling of belonging to the gang, this feeling that Manjit was following him like a puppy and that other boys in school would think twice before they said anything to a member of Manjit's mob.

When he got home, Manju was already there. She seemed to be waiting for him. Her face was expectant. 'What did you do in school?' she asked, her eyes darting all over him.

'Maths, English, drama, physics and GS,' he said. 'Do you know what the central problem of the Third World is?'

'Listen Pinder, I can only go out today if you tell Mummy you're coming with me. I'll give you sixty pence for the films if you want.'

'Keep your bloody money,' Bhupinder said. 'Besides, I want to watch *Star Trek*.'

He walked out of the room and went into his bedroom. Taking the pink envelope out of his pocket, he pushed a chair against the door and sat on it and opened the letter. It was a pink sheet of paper with a flower motif and it said in the corner in print: 'Khalsa Transport Co. "In God We Do Have Trust",' and then an address and phone number. The letter said:

My Respected Manjula,
You must forgive my writing this letter. I am asking your good brother Bhupinder to deliver the same. It is very good of you to say that we can meet each other far from other people's jealous eyes. I must tell you you are very beautiful, better than all film actress, and you must not believe all things that people in this East End are saying

about me especially Punjabi people because they are full of jealousy for good fortune. But I am not writing for bad purposes. You are more educated than me, but my father has a big truck company and your uncleji and your mataji all know my father and know he is a respectful person. I will ask your brother to make my introduction to your family and then we can stop meeting secretly. Still for just now I have to see and talk with you so please say when you are vacant and I will let you know through a letter via Bhupinder where to meet. This is just a quick note to let you know I am thinking of you always.

Yours
Manjit Singh

Bhupinder stared at the piece of paper. So she has seen him, he thought. He went to the kitchen and fetched a box of matches and locking himself in the lavatory he burnt the letter and the envelope and flushed it away.

For an hour he sat on his bed wondering what he should do. He could tell his mother that Manju was deceiving them, or he could confront her straight. He hit upon another plan. Manjit must be taught a lesson. The letter was obviously serious. He must do something. He went to the drawer and pulled out a sheet of paper. Then in his best hand he wrote:

Dear Manjit,
Meet me tomorrow in the corner of the school grounds at seven-thirty – your school, the place where there is a hole in the wall by the side.

Manju

He put the note in an envelope and put it into his school bag. As he thought of the details of the plan his hands began to sweat. He must kill Manjit or at least wound him seriously. He would lay an ambush for him, and yet he didn't know how it could be done. At least this way, Manjit would be alone and he had a chance. I'll have the element of surprise on my side, he thought, remembering the words their history teacher had used when talking about the British landings on the French coast. He'd have to go armed, he thought, and the idea gave him a weak shudder. He knew nothing about knives. Maybe a stick, a cricket bat or something on Manjit's head.

As he turned the problem over in his mind, Manju came into the room. 'Will you come with me?' she said, 'I just want to go down to Brick Lane and get some *jelabees* for after dinner.'

'I suppose you want to go into one of those filthy restaurants?' Bhupinder snarled.

'What's the matter with you Pindy, it'll only take fifteen minutes, and you like *jelabees* don't you?'

'I can't just now, I've got to write my letters and solve an important problem.'

'Don't talk rubbish, there's no one you can write letters to, or have you found yourself a little girlie?'

'Don't bother me, I've got business to do with some characters you don't know of.'

'You watch too much telly, I must tell Mummy to get you to bed before the gangster serials.' Manju could see that he wasn't going to help her.

'You can go by your bloody self, and don't think I don't know about your *jelabees*.'

'Mummy says you have to come with me.'

'You can fool Mummy, but you can't fool me,' Bhupinder replied. He sat at the table and pretended to be getting on with some work. He could hear Manju complaining that he wouldn't go with her and pleading to be allowed to go alone.

'Pinder, go with your sister,' his mother shouted.

'I'm not going anywhere with her,' Bhupinder shouted back. 'She disgraced me the other day in school, so she can paint up and stare in the mirror.'

He could hear his mother telling Manju that if she really wanted sweets so badly she'd make some herself, she had everything in the house. Bhupinder listened. He felt like letting Manju know that he knew she was deceiving their mother and that it wasn't sweets she was after, but it would only lead to a lot of crying and fuss. He would have to handle this thing a man's way. The burden was not his mother's to bear, it was his and it was heavy.

The letter lay like a little time bomb in his bag. The next day at school, he felt he ought to tear it up and throw it away and forget the whole business. How to deliver the letter?

The problem was solved for him by Manjit who appeared at the door of his form at lunch time. Bhupinder was putting away his stuff in his desk.

'You've had Bentley for geography?' Manjit said. 'He couldn't teach me a thing, poor fellow tried very hard.'

Bhupinder didn't feel like making school conversation. He took the envelope out of his bag and held it out to Manjit. Manjit grabbed hold of it and said, 'Hey thanks, I'll talk to you after lunch.' Then he was gone.

Now the whole thing had been put in motion. After school, Bhupinder went to examine the appointed spot. He hadn't exactly challenged Manjit to a duel, but he felt something of the excitement of having put out a challenge. There were boys playing penny-up against the broken wall in the corner of the playground and

Bhupinder thought it would look suspicious if he prowled around looking for a good place to hide and spring an ambush. He would come early and mark out The territory. There'd be nobody about and he could leap out from the shadows and deliver a few blows before Manjit even realised what was going on.

He went through the breach in the wall. The streets around this side of the school were derelict and boarded up, waiting for demolition. At seven-thirty they would certainly be empty.

He decided that he'd take a stick and tie a metal spike to it. It wasn't like carrying a knife, you couldn't kill a man with a stick, but you could make him beg for mercy. The problem was of course that he couldn't make his preparation or build his lethal weapon at home.

He skulked about his bedroom for a couple of hours. At six he changed into a sweater and his heaviest pair of boots and told his mother that he was going down to Inder's to fetch a text book.

He sped out of the house and made his way by the back streets to the deserted block. There was a lot of garbage about. He could certainly pick up a stick and string and anything else he wanted here. Even if he didn't win against Manjit, he thought, the other would have to respect his guts and that would make him leave Manju alone. It must have been near seven when he finally found a light metal pipe and decided it would be sufficient. He didn't want to cut the enemy too badly. He approached the breach in the wall and looked about. As he had anticipated, there was no one, not a stray cat about. Somewhere in the evening sky he could hear voices, the beat of a reggae record thumping through the thickening air. Just opposite the school wall were the empty houses, gutted and bare as skeletons. He could go in there.

Bhupinder walked into one of them and took up what he thought was a good position. He could see the breach in the wall and he couldn't be seen. He'd dash out and do his dirty work as Manjit stood around, or sat down on the spilt bricks. His boots crunched against the broken plaster and brick in the house. It was getting dark and he tried to ease himself into a position of complete silence. He could hear his own breath. Half an hour passed and no one came, no footsteps, no sound. He felt his body tightening as it did when he was about to jump into the cold water of a swimming pool. Inside the warm huddle of the sweater he was cold. And still no one came. It must be past seven-thirty now, Bhupinder thought. Maybe Manjit wasn't coming, maybe he'd seen through the challenge and wasn't man enough to accept it.

Just as he was thinking this, Bhupinder heard the rumble of a car engine and saw the lights of the car picking out a path in the deserted street. The car slowed down and stopped on the opposite side a few metres from where Bhupinder was hidden.

He's come in a car, Bhupinder thought. Why hadn't he thought of that? What should he do now? He waited to see if Manjit would get out of the car. He couldn't see into it from where he was and it was getting dark fast. He waited. The car door didn't open. Ten minutes passed and they seemed like an eternity to Bhupinder. He must do something. He put his head round the open doorway. The car's lights were switched off and he was sure the person in the car couldn't see him. He walked towards it. He'd call out for Manjit to climb out of his armour plating and face him like a man.

'Manjit,' he said, stepping forward, 'come out. It's me.'

Bhupinder stood in the middle of the road, his heart beating uncontrollably. Nothing happened. He walked closer to the car and bent down to the window to look in. On the front seat were two people, clutching each other, sprawling under the level of the windshield, the man on top of the woman. Bhupinder turned, not knowing what to do. It was an awful mistake.

The window of the car came down. 'Oi, you, mate, what the hell do you want?' a voice said, and the man's head poked out of the window.

'Not you,' Bhupinder said. 'I thought....'

'Well don't think, mate. Does a man have to go to the North Pole to get a little privacy?'

Bhupinder turned and walked away. Then he began to run. Just as he got to the corner of the derelict street, where it joined the main road, another car pulled into the street. He thought he saw Manjit at the wheel, but it was no use turning round now. As he made his way home he felt, well, if Manjit really wanted to take up his challenge he would have been there on time.

In a way he was disappointed. He had never been in a hand to hand fight before, at least not a serious one. He could remember when a boy in his primary school had set upon him and banged his head on the paving stones four times after sitting on him. That was a memory of having lost, and he had now lost the chance to have won. He would have proved himself, he was sure, and yet it was terrible. What would the man in the car think? That he had been prowling around trying to get a peep at lovers? It brought a blush to his cheeks.

He looked back, half expecting to see Manjit following him. He didn't want that. This way, at least he could feel that his challenge had been refused, or that Manjit had seriously thought that Manju was offering to meet him and had turned her down. Either way the problem was solved. Walking home, he remembered he'd told his mother that he was going to Inder's for a text book. He hurriedly stopped over at Inder's place and picked up a book.

'You look like you've seen a ghost,' Inder said.

'No, my mother will be a bit worried. If it's after eight she thinks the world has closed shop.'

He walked now with his head high and his step light. The burden had gone, he had somehow proved to himself that, even if he was terrified of disturbing the lovers in the car, he hadn't been scared of Manjit. Perhaps men only fight to prove to themselves they aren't afraid, to unload their dread, he thought.

He opened the door and as he entered his mother said, 'Where's Manju?'

'How should I know?'

'I sent her after you to Inder's. I thought you'd got into some talk with him, and you haven't even eaten this evening.'

'What time did you send her?' Bhupinder asked.

'About seven. You went out and said you'd be getting a book.'

'She'll be back,' Bhupinder said. 'You shouldn't have sent her after me, I can look after myself.'

'What could have happened to her? Are you sure you went to Inder's?'

Bhupinder looked at the clock on the mantelpiece. It was nearly eight-thirty.

'Look Mum,' he said in Punjabi. 'We're both grown up now. How old do you imagine we are? We don't have to go chasing around after each other. She can go where she damn well likes, I'm not running around town looking for her. She's a big girl now, you shouldn't worry about her. This house needs some new rules.' And then, seeing the pained expression on his mother's face, he added, 'Maybe she's gone round to her friend's after. She's seventeen, you know. Does a girl have to go to the North Pole to get some privacy?'

2 Pushy's Pimples

Samir and Pushpa sometimes called their father 'Daddy',
and they sometimes called him *'Pitaji'* according to
Indian custom. It depended on his mood. If he was
angry, or lecturing them about how Indian girls and
Indian boys should behave or not behave, how they
could so easily spoil his good name in the town, then
they said 'Yes, *Pitaji*', 'No *Pitaji*'. But if he came home
from the shop with presents for them, or when he
announced that the family were all going to the Hindi
films on Sunday, or to their uncle's place in Southall,
or if he was just plain nice and didn't insist on switch-
ing off the late night movie and ordering them up to bed,
then they called him 'Daddy'.

They knew he preferred the English word, especially
in front of white customers in the shop. His face would
compose itself in pride when he was called 'Daddy';
especially if it was Pushpa. He would ask her to get the
extra bottle of milk from the fridge in the back for a
late and regular customer and his eyes would shine with
pride when she replied in her London accent.

Pushpa was still the baby of the family and got most
of their dad's attention. Samir, now that he was in
college and Pushpa was still in school, was out and
about with his mates, and he didn't care. Girls need
that extra bit of care, especially Indian girls, he thought.

When Daddy passed his driving test there was general rejoicing at home. He would at last be able to drive them all to Leicester to his brother's place, and they could see their cousins over the weekend. He'd been promising the trip since he bought the van and began driving lessons with the Recommended School of Motoring. Samir was happy about that. He always said to Pushpa that their dad was tight and he was only taking them up by car because he wanted to save on the rail fares.

Pushpa, whom her friends at school called Pushy, should have been just as delighted. She had been looking forward to seeing Reena and Geeta, her twin cousins who were the same age as she was. She'd spent her childhood with them in the big house in Baroda, in India before they all came over to England. She loved being with the twins. They were the only ones in the family who understood all the things that were on her mind. Better than her English friends, and better than all the other Indian girls she knew. They met regularly at half-term and in the holidays, when they came down to London and Pushy showed them around. This time it was to be different. Their uncle, the twins' father, had written to say that since they'd be doing their CSEs that summer and had extra classes in the holidays, they had better stay in Leicester, and that they wouldn't come down to London. There was an important reason why Pushy didn't want to go with the family this particular weekend. She now had to make an excuse. She waited till she got her dad alone in the front room.

'Daddy, I can't go.'

'Everybody's going,' he said, lifting his eyes from the Gujerati newspaper he always settled into after work.

'But I can't, Miss Burntwood has got my ticket and

we're going to A *Midsummer Night's Dream*. I can't
miss it.'

'Too many dreams,' he said.

'It's not a dream, silly,' Pushy said. 'It's a play by
Shakespeare and it's on our syllabus and we have to go.'

Pushy was pleading. She was amazed at the ease with
which she told him this lie. She hadn't exactly planned
the story, but once she got going it came to her. He
can't find out, he'll never find out, she was thinking,
and when the real reason for her wanting to stay blotted
out the lie in her mind, a stony lump of spit gathered
in her mouth. When you tell a lie you have to swallow
a lump to clean your mouth out. Her hands began to
sweat. This was the first step.

'I'll ask your mother if you can be left alone for two
days. It's too long by yourself. How can I face my brother
and say I've left Pushpa all alone in the house?'

'I won't be by myself, Daddy. I'll be with Miss
Burntwood on Friday and then I'll go down to Chacha's
on Saturday by train.' She looked at his face and knew
that it was working. 'It's on my O level syllabus. All
the kids in the class are going.'

Mr Patel shouted across to his wife in the kitchen.
Pushpa wasn't going with them. There was no comment
from the kitchen. Pushpa knew that it wasn't the sort
of argument that her mother would get into.

Pushpa's heart began to beat faster and she ran up
to her room. It was at the back of the house on the first
floor. If her mother saw her face, she thought, she'd
know that something was on Pushpa's mind. She was
sharp, you couldn't lie to her.

Pushy went up to the mirror on her dressing table.
She stuck her tongue into her cheek to push the skin

out. She looked at the pimples on her face. They made a heavy pink rash from under her eyes to the bottom of her jaw bone, on both sides. Like a volcano, she thought, exploding like a volcano. She was beyond crying about it. For the last year she'd fought a battle with these pimples, this stain on her otherwise beautiful face. She saw that the door was shut and pulled the tube of Skintex out from under her mattress and gently rubbed smears of cream on to the ugly spots. She hated them, they weren't part of her body, they were an invasion. At last she'd have the chance to wipe them out. All-out attack, she repeated in a whisper. She'd heard a man on the telly say it. Pushy knew the Skintex was no good. Some mornings she woke up having dreamt that the curse had gone, but she would look in the mirror and see that it was redder and more bloody-looking than ever. She'd tried everything, and still the spots seemed to multiply. It was like those science fiction movies in which some fungus or plant or vine or something begins to creep all over the face of the earth and no power can stop it. She'd bombarded her face with lotions from every chemist she knew of. She'd written, without letting her dad know, and under a false name, to the beauty parlours and the women's magazines. Nothing. It would bring tears to her eyes. If she had just one wish, like the girls in the fairy stories did, that would be it. To lose this blight. She longed to have the smooth silky skin of the girls in the magazines, the girls in the street, the girls at school, the girls on telly, that girls anywhere and everywhere seemed to have. Except her. Maybe there was some truth to her mother's belief that sins in your past life have to be punished in your present life. She wanted to cast off this skin, if necessary to cast off her body, like a snake or a spirit, and coil into something else.

Everyone noticed. One girl in school had said that Indians bring disease into the country, and even though Pushy knew it was just something in the class discussion, she wanted to bury her face in the desk. For the white girls, having spots and pimples meant something else. They never made fun of her directly, but they had a joke about pimples. Denise had said something that gave her a hint about it. It was awful to think of, and yet she'd been thinking about it. A hundred times since.

She asked Michelle, her best friend in school, to explain what it was they were giggling about. When she was alone with Michelle she could ask her anything, about bras and underwear and the things she didn't dare ask her mother. When they were with their other classmates, Pushy knew that Michelle wanted her to pretend to know as much as anyone else. Michelle didn't want them to know, she felt, that it was she who told Pushy about boys and sex and private girl things, what she called 'the facts of life'. When they were alone Michelle wasn't shy about these things, even though Pushy blushed when she used certain words.

'Don't be so damn silly,' Michelle would say. 'You have to know haven't you? You can't remain innocent all your life, can you?'

It was true, Pushy thought, and thank God for Michelle and her concern to steer her out of innocence. Still, about this latest thing, Pushy wasn't sure. It frightened her and she preferred not to think about it. She wasn't sure that she'd even understood Michelle correctly.

'It's in your blood,' Michelle said, 'hormones and that. They get to boiling and then you've got to let the heat out. Once your blood gets the heat out, then you'll be all right. Married women don't get pimples, see?'

Pushy tried to test this theory on the street, but she had no way of knowing who was married and who wasn't. She looked from their ring fingers to their faces. She thought of all the teachers who weren't married and she pointed out to Michelle that none of them had acne. 'Them teachers,' Michelle said, 'the amount of heat they let out they ought to have cold sores instead.' Pushy dropped the subject but she wanted to know if Michelle was serious. When they were walking in the park at break she brought it round to pimples again.

'You should try it,' Michelle said. 'After all if you've used Tampax, you know the job's already done so I don't know what all the fuss is about. Look at me, I don't have any pimples. I reckon most of the girls in our year have had it, at least once. Except Annette and she's a weed.'

Pushy thought of Annette. She was a plump girl in their form and she was the only white girl who had a faint trace of spots on her face. She and Annette, they were marked, she thought. Everyone knew.

Pushy knew that Michelle had done all sorts of things. She always told Pushy about what her boyfriend and she had done the previous evening, and how he'd wanted it and how she hadn't been in the mood.

'You should stand up to your dad. After all, it isn't India, and the old man had better change his little ways.'

Pushy didn't want to tell Michelle that it wasn't her dad. Boys never asked her out. There was a magic circle of Indianness around her which stopped a boy from getting close. There were the boys at the Asia Club, but they were Indian boys and knew that drinking coke at the bar and sitting together at concerts was as far as they could go. Sometimes they took some of the girls for a spin in their cars, but they never asked her. Pimples again. She didn't blame them.

Then Michelle had made her an offer. She said that if one day Pushy could get away, Ron's friend Steve would like to take her out.

'You wouldn't mind trying it with him, would you, he's ever so nice. And he's Ron's best mate.'

Pushy didn't know what 'trying it' meant, but she suspected that Michelle just meant going out with him, maybe hold hands, maybe allow him to kiss her. Ron was Michelle's boyfriend and he'd brought Steve to the fifth-year dance. They, Ron and Steve, worked together, and since they didn't know the other kids in school, they had formed a foursome under Michelle's management. Pushy told Steve she didn't know how to dance, and he said he didn't care, it was just an excuse to grab hold of girls anyway.

Of course Pushy was flattered that Steve wanted to see her again. He had asked Michelle about the 'Paki girl'. Michelle said it in a matter-of-fact way and added, 'He's not prejudiced or nothing, just a bit flash and carries on like that, but he really fancies you.'

When Pushy told Michelle that the house was going to be empty that weekend, she hoped that Michelle remembered about Steve. She didn't want to ask outright. 'Can't face Leicester and all that Indian family scene,' she said. Michelle understood all right.

'Right,' she said, 'what the stars foretell. We'll go out in Ron's car and end up at your place. Don't be scared, it'll be all right. All you have to do is relax and let him talk and I'll take care of everything else.'

Pushy knew what Michelle meant by 'everything else'. She got a sinking feeling in her stomach. Babies, she thought. If you have it you can get pregnant, but Michelle obviously knew how to avoid that.

Pushy didn't give Michelle a definite answer, but she knew that Michelle would now plan the whole thing. She looked in the mirror when she got home from school on Thursday. Mirror, mirror on the wall.... Pushing back her long hair, she thought, yes, I've got nice eyes, and delicate small ears and my skin is soft brown and ... her fingers touched her cheeks. Tomorrow, she thought.

'Pushpa,' her dad called.

'I'm doing my homework, Daddy.'

'We are motoring tomorrow so we are sleeping early,' he shouted.

'Blimey,' she heard Samir saying, 'you'd think we were going round the world in eighty days, the way you carry on.'

Pushy sat late into the night after the house was dark and everyone else had gone to bed. Her family must never find out, she thought over and over again. And then her mind turned to Steve. But she didn't think of him as he was, she thought of him as a sort of ghost, but not white in colour, brushing against her body and his hand on her cheek. What Michelle said must be true, it had to be true. If she did this one thing, just once, she might get rid of the pimples forever. It was as if her prayers had been answered, but not by God she thought, by the Devil. It didn't matter; she was determined to do it. She'd shut her eyes. Would it be

38

worth it? What had she to lose? What if she found she liked it? Could you become addicted to sex like an animal, or like people get addicted to cigarettes, and then not be able to live without it? If Daddy found out he'd kill her, he couldn't stand that, it would be the end.

On Friday morning she left for school thinking that she'd tell Michelle it was all off. The morning passed. Pushy kept looking at Michelle all through the English lesson. In the lunch break she went up to her.

'Michelle, about this evening, I don't want to do it.'

'You're a baby. You don't have to do anything you don't want. I'll be there to tell him off if he gets out of control.'

How could he get out of control, Pushy asked herself, would he tear her clothes off, and his face get fixed in a cruel mask? No, she couldn't do it.

'C'mon it'll be a nice evening, he may never ask you again, you know.'

When the bell rang at the end of the afternoon and Michelle and Pushy walked as usual to the corner together, Michelle touched her on the cheek with one finger and said, 'The Secrets of Sex from Mademoiselle Michelle. Look, it'll be all right, we'll just have a spin in the car.'

There was no one at home when Pushy got back. Dad had said they'd make an early start to avoid driving in the dark. Pushy felt cold in the house. She put on the front-room fire and she went through all the rooms checking to see if they were tidy. She went to the corner of the street and bought a few cans of coke and some beer. She had to go through with it now, if only to show Michelle that she wasn't as babyish as Michelle imagined. She wouldn't allow them to stay all night. That way she wouldn't be actually sleeping with a man. She may allow him to touch her or kiss her or something in the front room, but she wouldn't even let him know where her bedroom was. Michelle could go up there with Ron if she liked. If only she could have the same attitude as Michelle had to men. Life would be so much easier. But that would mean her father would have to have different attitudes, and Samir, and her mother, and that was impossible.

It wasn't that she was innocent, she knew everything. Miss Burntwood had talked about it in class, in front of the boys. She'd even said dirty words, the one with 'f' and the one beginning with 'c', and she said they were perfectly good words because D. H. Lawrence used them, only you had to know when and where to use them. The girls had laughed. They listened carefully to her. There was not a whisper in class and some of them said afterwards that she was a frustrated old cow, she must have had it once in her lifetime and was celebrating the anniversary of the event by talking filth in class. Pushy liked Miss Burntwood, and thought that the girls were just jealous of her. After all, she was being frank and teaching them what she was paid to teach. Still, it was no good Miss B saying that it didn't matter if a girl was not a virgin, that many girls lost their virginity through physical exercise and horse-riding and sometimes naturally during periods. Everyone knew men didn't have respect for girls who were too easy. If an Indian boy ever found out about a girl not being a virgin, he wouldn't marry her. Yet there was no sure way of knowing, a man could never be certain, and mature people should always be honest about their experiences.

I'll never be honest about this, Pushy thought, I'll never tell the man I marry. I'll do it once and try and forget it. Time dulls the memory she had heard, also that time cures all wounds, except her stupid pimples. If she carried them around, nobody would marry her anyway. By some miracle this boy Steve fancied her. Maybe she would eventually marry an Englishman, maybe even him. He and Ron were partners in a moving business, they drove a truck and were making their way, Michelle said.

If it didn't work out and he just wanted her for her body, she would have a bath after and forget him. She'd drink some beer and then she could say that she didn't know what he'd done to her and it wouldn't be her fault. She'd pretend she didn't remember a thing.

As she dressed she looked at herself in the mirror, naked, whole. She'd let the man who married her have a good look. Steve wasn't to be given the impression that she was what the English girls called a 'slag'. If she let him, only *if*, then she'd let her skirt down just a little and shut her eyes and he could do the rest. As she climbed into her only non-uniform skirt, she practised loosening the buttons and her heart thumped like a drum.

Ron and Steve were already at Michelle's place when she got there. They suggested they go to a pub, and when they got there they left the girls with Babychams and went off to play darts. Steve had been very attentive to her in the car. He was tall and had short blond hair and he showed her where he'd had his ear pierced to put on an ear-ring.

'Long John Silver with a brass,' Ron said, but Pushy didn't get the joke and Michelle coiled up to him as he was driving and tittered. He didn't touch her, even though Ron and Michelle were kissing each other as though they each needed artificial respiration every time they'd stop at the lights and when they climbed in and out of the car.

'He says he really wants to,' Michelle said to Pushy when the boys were out of earshot. Even hearing that made Pushy's stomach go funny. Michelle was dressed as usual for the evening with a tight, low-cut T-shirt and jeans. 'We can go round to Pushy's place,' she said, as though the boys didn't know. 'There's no one there, her family are away.'

'I'm a removal man,' Steve said when they got talking.

'Girls' knickers mainly,' Ron said. But Steve didn't even laugh. He kept his distance and made funny remarks of his own. He was very clever, Pushy thought, and wondered if he really fancied her or whether Michelle had just told her that so she and Ron could have a place for the night. She was surprised at herself when she found herself wishing with all her heart that he would touch her, just to show that he did fancy her, that she was not repulsive to him, that he could look past her pimples with his gorgeous green eyes.

Steve was talking to her about the Indian films he'd seen. He said he went because he used to have a school friend from the East End called Pat, and did she know him? But he found the people in the films beautiful. Then he turned to talking about how he'd been with this friend Pat to curry places and Pat had made him eat something which burnt the tongue out of his head and made his body feel like it was on fire. Indians must be very hot-blooded, he said, and Pushy wondered if Michelle had told him anything at all about her problem.

'I never eat curries,' Pushy said. 'That's only in restaurants.'

'I told Pat it was a black power plot to kill whitey,' Steve said. Pushy's mood was slowly changing from being worried to being amused and very interested in how his mind worked and how he acted out with his hands the stories he told himself.

Michelle directed Ron to Pushy's house. It was almost twelve by the time they'd finished driving around and Pushy was relieved, because it would mean the neighbours would be asleep. She was thinking that she felt a bit drunk anyway and she wouldn't have to pretend so hard. I'm going to let him, she thought. And then it struck her that he may not want to. As the car stopped she felt herself breaking into a sweat. This was it. They were out of the car. Her feet seemed to move automatically. She felt Steve's hand next to hers and his fingers, without warning, reached for hers. She pulled her hand away.

'Not here, the neighbours,' she said, and he smiled and nodded vigorously. Pushy walked up to the house, wanting to seem casual. She'd put the reading lamp on the floor so anyone passing wouldn't see the front room lit.

Gaskarth Road was deserted. She must be silent in case the snooping neighbours ... walls have ears.

The blood was pounding in her temples. Once they were inside, everything would work like in a play. If I don't do it now, I'll never do it, I have to, I have to, she kept thinking and a knot gathered in her tummy. She pulled the key out of her handbag and put it in the lock. Just as she did that a light went on behind the curtain in the upstairs room. She heard footsteps inside the house. Michelle and Ron saw it too.

Pushy's heart sank.

'Someone's doing your place,' Ron said.

The front door opened before Pushy could push it and Mr Patel's figure, in the act of reaching for the hallway light stood framed in the door. He took in the scene at a glance.

'It's twelve o'clock,' was all he said.

Pushy's mind raced and the words came without her thinking.

'Michelle and Miss Burntwood's brother brought me home from her place,' she said.

Pushy didn't know if Ron and Steve would understand.

'Thanks Michelle, thank you Mr Burntwood,' she said, turning to them, telegrams of panic in her eyes, her face trying to keep cool. Michelle nudged Ron who was the only one whose puzzlement showed in his face.

'Not at all, Pushpa, and now I'd better see the other young lady home,' Steve said, and Pushy noticed that he'd changed his accent and put on his best posh voice. Her eyes said thank you, but Steve was smiling at Mr Patel. 'Very nice meeting you, Pushpa. Goodnight Mr Patel,' he said.

Pushy watched the performance as if she were watching something on television. Her father was uncertain, but he muttered a goodnight.

Samir came downstairs in his pyjamas as they shut the door behind them. 'You should have seen it,' he said. 'Dad was dead scared of the motorway. He stopped three lanes of traffic single-handed.' Mr Patel grunted and went upstairs. 'How was the play?' Samir asked.

'I liked it,' Pushy said.

'We're going by train tomorrow. The old man won't save on the fares anyway, he's decided to keep off the motorway. It was really funny, he went five kilometres up and came right back. You can come, can't you?'

'I'd like to see Reena and Geeta,' Pushy said, 'but old Burntwood is having us round to discuss the play tomorrow and I haven't decided whether to go or not.'

3 East End at Your Feet

A *Tale of Two Cities*, that's what I'd call it if the blink-ing title hadn't been bagged by somebody else. I re-member the story, and Miss Mullins' voice reading and the girls listening as though they were in love with every rascal whose head was chopped. I remember the part about the guillotine, and catching the head in a bucket. She told us that the fellow what invented that got the chop himself. Must have felt weird, like getting your hand caught in the mouse trap that you're putting cheese in for the little devils. No, not quite like that, more like the other story she told us about a fellow who invented a maze and put a monster in the centre of it, and then got trapped in it himself and couldn't find the way out. I feel like that, only I didn't invent the damn maze, only my own thoughts. I invent those all the time and get lost in them.

Charles Dickens wrote the first story of that name, about Paris and London, but my story can't be about Paris because I never got further than Boulogne on a school trip. I remember that trip, drinking one whisky after another in the bar on the boat and all the lads running about the streets and playing silly-boys with the mademoiselles we met. 'How about a bit of the *autre*,' and all that crap. And then one of them says to me : 'Go on Cashy, show them the rope trick, pull it out and make it stand up by whistling *God Save the Prime Minister* in Indian.' I never took no notice. I used to think them things myself, but I never said them.

My story's got to be about Bombay and London. Not that I know much about Bombay, I haven't even started school here yet. My uncle says I'm the head of the household, but I feel like its arse, everyone sitting on me and kicking me around. Not my mum and Sheila and Shobha, my sisters. They just mope around and my mum cries, God she can cry, she's a champion at it. Every day there's priests in the house. They turn up regular as the milkman, and start muttering their nonsense, and then Mum cries even more. She starts howling and my aunts come and say 'There, there' and bull like that.

I can't take it. Not that I'm not sad or hardhearted or anything, but I prefer to be with myself, and I sit on the balcony and watch the seagulls and the cars crawling along the sea road. Sometimes there are sails out on the water, fishermen, the same blokes who pull their nets up on the beach and dry out kilometre on kilometre of the stinking Bombay Ducks. If the breeze is this way, the pong comes in and you have to shut the doors and go in.

It's Saturday, I checked it on the calendar in Grandad's room. Nobody knows what day of the week it is here. If you have something to do then you count the days to the weekend, because you always want them to hurry up, or to slow down. Days are like money, my dad used to say. They are like loose change now that I've got nothing to do but spend them.

The lads are in the park now. We put down our jackets as goalposts and the teams divide automatically.

Same teams from day to day and week to week. I'm the best goalkeeper in Hackney, I reckon. Juniors, I'm talking about, I'm not that big-headed to think I'm professional standard. Not yet. Maybe never now. But I play in the first eleven for the school. I never let one past the day we played Dalston Grammar, even though they said it was a hard team and they'd score off us as easy as giving candy to a baby. (I like to say it that way, because babies are getting tough nowadays and you can't *take* stuff off them as easy as you could.) This big black bloke was playing centre forward for them and he charged the ball right up. He was hanging around and wouldn't take a shot, wanted to bring it in safe. If I was ref, I'd have given him offside at least three times, but them old geezers are blind, at least blind to what grammar school teams do on the field. I fell on the ball at his feet. I took a dive, like I was going off the deep end. He kicked me in the mouth but I'd got the ball. I showed my lip, cut and bleeding, to Mr Knights, our coach, at half time, but he said it was too late to do anything about it.

'Kashyap, boy, we've got to win this game, we want goals not hospital cards.'

'All right,' I said, 'all right.' I stopped him two more tries in the second half. He thought he could elbow it past me if he tempted me out of the goalposts. He tried to get his shoulder down and into my chest, but I jumped on the ball. I didn't care if he tossed me around like a bull with a rag stuck on its horns. The kids from our school went wild. They rushed on the pitch. 'These bastards want to play rugby,' Rob said to me. He was our full-back.

Mr Knights tells me he's going to send me for the West Ham trials. I can see myself in light blue and claret, those are our colours, and all the girls sending me messages through my mates. Sharon wants to go out with you, and are you coming to the fourth-year dance, because Diane fancies you? Nah, I've got the trials coming up and I've got to practice. Become impenetrable, like the bloody Wall of China past which nothing can get.

To be a good goalkeeper you have to practice. It's even harder to be good at than Kung Fu is, even though some blokes in our year reckon that that's the most difficult game. Skills. I reckon that's a load of cods, because no geezer's going to play fair with you just because you've got your black belt on. They're going to thump you first and look at your certificates after. That's if you're still alive. Best way is to get a stick or a chain, or a knife, or best of all a gun, like all the villains in the East End. I heard once that the Kray brothers hired a tank to attack a lad that grassed on them. They'd heard he had a machine gun and didn't want to take no risks. They drove it right down Mile End Road and the public thought it was army carrying out manoeuvres. You hear a lot of stories like that in London and I reckon half of them are only three-quarters true or half true. Which makes the level of truth in London half of half, or three-quarters of half, whatever that is. That's more than Bombay, I can tell you that, at least from the things that have happened here. My uncle said at the airport that it was a modern building they lived in. When we get here, it's all falling to bits, and he said there was beach in front of it, but the bloody rocks he was talking about are nearly a kilometre away even though you can see them from the balcony if you've got your specs on.

He was going to look after us, he says, when we get off the plane in Bombay, all sleepy and full of food because they give you a meal every half hour on them flights. He said to my mum not to worry about a thing and next day he brings in these sharp lawyer blokes to get me to sign all sorts of papers. They put a cross against an empty space and say sign here. My mum looks on and says I'd better sign where my uncle says, and I tell her to get away from the papers or they'll have to put them in the drier before they can use them in court or whatever they're doing. The lawyer blokes, all in black coats like scarecrows, all look at my uncle as though I was an animal or something getting out of control.

These lawyers don't look as smart as the one I had when I was up in the magistrates' court in Bow. That customer was really flash. I was sitting on this plush chair in his waiting room with his secretary typing away with a mini-skirt covering what was good above her blue tights. She says, 'Put your jacket on before going in to see Mr Big himself.'

'I'm hot,' I said.

She looked me up and down and said, 'Impatient to get in the cooler?' Smart bird.

'Why don't you go on telly?' I said. 'You'd run Frankie Howerd out of business.'

The solicitor says, 'I'm going to take a statement on the tape-recorder, but before we switch that on, I want you to tell me if you actually intercepted the merchandise.'

I said I don't know and he began speaking to me like I was deaf mute, encouraging me to lip-read him.

'I'm sorry sir, I may be Indian, but I speak perfectly good English, but I haven't swallowed a dictionary and

I was just wondering if you'd clarify your inquiry.' I like that: 'clarify your inquiry'.

'You're a cocky young fellow.' If he'd said that to Mel or Tony, they would have fallen about.

I was given a year's probation, we all were. Mel had actually driven the van full of sugar packets, millions of 'em, and he was charged heavy and sent down to Stamford House.

'That's where you'll end up, and the game won't touch you, they won't have a con in any of the teams from here to Lisbon,' Mr Knights said. He was giving me a lecture on going straight for the sake of the game. Now I don't know where Lisbon is, but I guess it's far enough for me not to want banning from here to there, so I said I'd go straight. And apart from nicking sweets and a few things from Woolworths for Christmas, I never joined the lads in the game. Knighty said I had a chance, and I hung on to it like they say a drowning man holds on to a straw. Only I never figured out how straw got on the sea in the first place. It's all a load of bollocks – I could make up better proverbs than that. Like spitting on a forest fire, I said once. I got a pat on the back for that. One remark like that and the dumb teachers remember it till the end of the term. 'Kashyap shows creative talent in his English lessons.'

'What's that?' my dad asked, looking at the report.

'I'm good at poetry,' I said. But my dad obviously thought that poetry was only good for poofs. Chances are he never knew what poofs were. But he knew what mattered. His eye would check on the physics and chemistry and maths reports.

'Your father had a lot of hope and ambition for you,

Kashyap. You must try and live up to his faith in you, and fulfil his life's wishes.'

But I was thinking about my own life's wishes. I wanted that blue and claret shirt, West Ham forever. If I'd been given two more years in London, that's what I'd have done.

I don't know much Hindi, but I have to speak to my grandad in Hindi 'cause he don't know nothing else. I'm young enough to learn, but he ain't, and that's the reason I suppose I could learn to like Bombay. They say I will, I'll forget London. It's not London I'm worried about, it's just the whole idea of changing your life. At my age kids don't normally have plans for their lives, but you can see how you're going to grow up, you have a pretty fair idea. Now it's India and starting all over again, with friends, with the language and even getting used to the stinks.

I used to pretend I couldn't speak Hindi when I was with the lads. We are on a street corner and the rest of them are deciding whether we ought to go up the West End and tease the prostitutes and play the pin balls. We're outside the café and nobody has a penny on them. A Paki geezer comes along. He's got this fuzzy hat and a long coat and tight trousers. I can tell he's a Muslim, but they can't. I don't see him approaching. He stops by John and he says, quite polite like, 'Could you please directing me, one address ...' and all this, and he sticks out a grubby little bit of paper. Only one problem, it's not in the East End. The address he's got scribbled is down in Blackheath or some place. So John says to him he can't go straight there and Mel says, 'Yeah, you have to turn yourself at the corners,' putting on what he thinks is an Indian accent. Then he says, 'Shall we roll him?'

The rest of them are looking at me. They were staring in my face to see how I was taking it, because Mel wasn't thinking when he said that, just naturally taking the mick. So John says, 'Shut your yapping mouth, you Irish git, so what if the geezer's not English, you got something against Cash and his lot?' And then he hands the bloke over to me. OK, so I'm Indian and I go up to the bloke and talk to him in Hindi, whatever I can manage and I tell him to go down to the Elephant and then take a 53 bus. He smiles all over and puts out his hand and taps me on the shoulder to show he's grateful.

When he's gone, Mel says, 'Say something again in Indian.'

'Not for you,' I says.

'Go on, Cash, I didn't mean it, you know I was just larking about.'

'That could have been my dad,' I said, 'and how was he to know you're Mr Humorous himself?'

'Keep it on,' he says, 'keep it on, son, it's windy today.'

So I cussed him with all the Hindi swear words I could think of, and they all fell about holding their guts and doubling up right there on the pavement. I taught them a few of the best, and they went around shouting them at all the Indian faces they met in the street and at school in the next few days.

I said I get the stink of the drying Bombay Duck and with it I can imagine the smell of cod in batter at the local chippy. That's the worst of it. What I wouldn't give for a real fry-up from down Kingsland Road. It's vegetarian food in my grandad's house. All *daal* and rice and *bhendu* and enough yogurt to drown an elephant in. Ugh, yoghurt down your throat three times a day, or starve. I can't complain. It isn't even our house, and Mum's in mourning so I feel selfish if I even think of my tum, but I can't help it.

My uncle keeps telling me to think about taking up my studies where I left off, but he doesn't know that I never left off, I hardly got started. I'll confess that I'm worried about that now, I keep thinking of O levels or whatever they have here, and how I wouldn't get a job without them here. It's not like London where you can go on the dole, there isn't any dole here. They just let you die in the street, them loving Indians, and I've seen it, I tell you. There's people sleep on the streets all over the city and some of them are just skin, like plastic bags stretched over their bones.

My uncles say they'll look after us now. They're always in and out of the house and Christ I have to remember all their names and the right names to call everyone each time they ask you something. Sometimes I feel I have to get out, because all these uncles just talk about 'the future' all the time like it was their favourite subject. I make excuses to get out. I say I'll get a new toothbrush and they say they'll send the servant out for one. So I say he won't know the West Ham colours and they look at me as though I'm barmy. It must seem a bit doolally looking for West Ham coloured toothbrushes in Bombay. I get down the elevator like a shot. Blokes always touching their heads in *salaam* here. My uncle's a big shot. Dad used to tell us about him sometimes in London, say he'd go into partnership with him once he'd saved enough money. You'll never save a bean, we used to say and I believed it.

I am down in the park. It isn't much of a park, just a huge empty space with a few palm trees tucked in a corner. Plenty of people about, all playing cricket and chucking stones about. There's a game of football too. If you're a goalie, you can't just ask for a game, everyone has to trust you before the game starts. It's not like playing anywhere else on the field, where you can join in and tackle someone and dribble past them and do your stuff. These kids are playing without shoes.

If I get into a school I'll get in their team. I asked about football. They don't even have a blooming league. You've got to join the army if you want to play football; it's good exercise, good for the young to take exercise. That's my grandad, a bit behind the times, but what can you expect? He's never been out of Bombay in his life.

'Humans are the same everywhere.' That's Miss Mullins. She thought she ought to feel sorry for me. 'You've taken it very well. I was wondering what had happened to you. I've been to India and it's absolutely wonderful. It'll be better for you of course. They're your own people. All this confusion of the East End will disappear. You will think of us, as we shall think of you, won't you?' And then the girls throwing their arms around me. 'Cashy, don't forget us now.' It was as if I'd stopped a hundred for West Ham juniors already.

I heard the Headmaster saying to Mullins when I was standing outside the door, 'He'll be better off, wisest thing.' He didn't say that to me. He said, 'Kashyap my boy, you've had one or two scrapes with the law but all is forgotten and we'll always be proud of you.'

It was only then I began to think about the whole thing, going away. Like dying, really. Mullins said confusion, but there was no confusion before. My dad was no big shot, he was a tailor and the confusion only started when he kicked it. Died, I mean.

He worked at one of them firms that made you do all the stitching and cutting and then took the profits and gave you twenty-five a week. Peanuts. And our house showed it. After he died, the hire purchase man came and took the telly and the fridge and the damned plastic covered couches in the front room.

'Leave that stuff alone,' I said.

The trucker said, 'Argue with the bailiff, mate, I'm doing my job.' I'd have laid one on him. Right, I'm smaller, but I'd have hurt him as much as he could damage me. But Mr Dayal, my dad's mate, he said to leave them, they had a right because my dad hadn't kept up the payments and we wouldn't need the things because we were packing up to go anyway.

It was two weeks before it was all over and fixed. The social workers came and all our Indian neighbours. They knew my parents but they wouldn't have anything to do with me and used to tell my dad to whip me and keep me in line like they did with their sons. He never beat me once, though. He lectured me, about how hard he'd worked, and how he'd saved money for three years to go home and get married.

'Was it worth it?' I used to ask, and he'd scowl at me and say that my mum was the jewel of the east.

'Ever seen a hundred-kilogram diamond?' I asked him, but he never hit me.

He said, 'Kashyap, Kashyap, all boys are disgraceful. It is their nature, but it is bad to joke with your elders.' I agreed with him. It wasn't him at all that bothered me. And it was all true about how he'd worked. I know

56

because he had a buttonhole machine at home and he'd do extra work after hours, and that meant till two in the bleeding morning, his fingers like Olympic spiders crawling all over that nifty machine. I told him there was better work for quick fingers to do. Actually, he knew all about me. When he looked at me with dark eyes it was as though he could see right through me. And he was proud of me, like they all are, proud of his eldest son.

They all stare at you in the same way. The beggars in the street, the people in the trains. Boy, they said the East End was a slum but anyone who says that ought to have a look at this place, even without glasses on. Half the houses aren't even houses, they're just tin and wood boards and stuff. Not our house. I'm sitting in the front room and the fan in the ceiling goes round like a helicopter, like the whole place is going to take off or maybe come crashing down, but my mum said it's been there for years and made the same noise before I was born. The flies aren't scared off by the racket it makes. They are my grandad's mates. His game is grabbing a few of them. He shows me how to grab them by bringing your palm up slowly and snatching at the air above them. I'm an expert now.

I go to school and I come back, and then out with my mates in the evening. I don't mind doing a few things for Mum in between, but after seven my time's my own. You should see the stuff they have on telly here, cor blimey, no *Kojak*, no *Kung Fu*. Not that I miss the telly. I miss the lads. It warn't nicking and that, leastways not always, sometimes it was just walking down the streets and chatting up the girls, or going up the youth club. And in our fourth year at school everyone begins thinking about jobs, then it's lectures and parents' meetings and everybody making up their minds. It's a miracle in that bunch. A thieving lot, Mel and John and Mo. Now Mo's going to drive his father's trucks. With a couple of trucks to back you, you can fart on O levels, he says. And John's going into the docks on account of his old man. And Gordy'll be a bloody butcher's assistant. Can't read so he'll be chopping out best New Zealand to someone who asked for English Lamb. He says he can tell by the colour. So Mo says, yeah, stamped with Union Jacks.

I never tell them I'm going to be a doctor. Dad goes on at me about it and I know he writes home regularly and always there's something to mention about how well I'm getting on with maths, even though I've torn my book up in front of the maths teacher and got sent home and suspended till Dad comes up and begs.

'I've never known any of your lot behave as badly as you do Kashyap, but Mr Knights here is willing to put in a good word for you, and only on his say-so we have agreed to give you a further chance to fit into our community.'

I couldn't give a monkey's for his community and all that, but I want to stay in the team, so I just swallow my pride, like a spoonful of castor oil that my grandad thinks is good for you. Makes you fart something rotten. My dad doesn't care for it, not the castor oil, the football I'm thinking of, and Knights says I stand a chance. I'm down in front of the net and the best shooters in the school taking shots with three balls and I'm diving and dancing like crazy, like a maniac with ants in his pants.

So I think to myself that even if he's not seen Indians like me, he hasn't seen them in his first eleven or in goal either. Sure, they play cricket, they do good maths, the teacher's pets. All crawling and in the sixth form, to be lawyers and accountants. Some from Uganda who are called Asians. With hair like poofs, trying to look like Brian Ferry or some crumb from the hall of fame. They'll never have the East End at their feet. You know, that's the saddest thing about it. All of them, crawlers, were looking to clear out from the East End. Go and work in the City and live in Kensington or some posh place and dress up in pinstripes and say 'toppung' and call their mates 'old chap'.

My dad wanted me dropped from the team, and he even came up and told old Knights, but Knights wanted to win the league so he says he'll keep his tidy mouth shut as long as I keep coming to practice. It used to come to me that the only way I would ever become a pro was if my dad died. I hate the thought now, but I'm being straight, and I'm even thinking it wasn't what I thought, I'm not Uri Geller or one of them magic blokes who can think things and they happen. That's what I thought when he refused to buy me my kit and Knighty had to beg it off of the school. It was rotten. I couldn't even take my cup home. John was on the team and he said your dad's a nutter, because his old man took his down the local to show his mates.

I heard a lot about India this and India that from my mum, but it was never my business, because I reckoned on dying a cockney. It's what fourteen years can do to you. I thought the East End would do for me like it did for my dad, when it choked him up and they brought him home on a stretcher and Mum and I spent the whole night at the hospital.

We sat in the corridor on a bench and I put my arm

round my mum. She was howling something terrible. The doctor comes in with a nurse with a face looking like half past six, and they call me aside. 'I'm awfully sorry.'

And I couldn't think of nothing to say so I says, 'It's not your fault.' Then I can't get my mum away from the doctor. She never touched a white man in her life, not even to take change in a shop, and she's hanging on to the doctor like she was drowning and he'd come in to save her. Talking Hindi and trying English and crying all the time. So he leaves her with the nurse. Brushes her off, his jaw drops down to his waist, he can't handle this mad Indian woman who's begging him to do something, do anything.

Then the crematorium and the priests and relatives I didn't know existed, and mutterings and prayers in the house, all streaming in from Leamington Spa and Bradford and God knows where, with all their grubby children, all wearing Bri-nylon shirts and saying what a good man he was as if they knew the first thing about my dad. And they vanish the next day and it rains and England is shutting down.

I go down to the firm where Dad used to work and the manager talks to me for a good half hour. They can't employ me, I'm too young. Just two years more, so I'd better do what my uncle says. He came all the way from India. Nothing for you here he says, cold climate no good. I'd have given my dad half my life if it could be done, just to stay in West Ham.

He could talk about the climate, it's like a bloody oven here and raining half the time. I'm sitting on the balcony and there's a blind beggar with a little girl guiding him. Letters from England. John says West Ham are playing

Leeds and West Ham are favourites for the Cup. They've dropped Clyde Best for the game, and the lads send their love and kisses. One day ... but no good thinking about that. The beggar's opened up his harmonium and his blind eyes looking like white marbles are pointed towards me. He's beginning to sing his song and the little girl is just standing there waiting to start wailing for money when he's past the first verse. I don't care much for Hindi songs, though some of the words are good. This one says,

'Go away, fly away, bird
Go to the home of singing choirs
There's nothing for you here, my beauty ...'
Or something like that. My Hindi's improving.

4 The China Set

My nan is much wiser than my dad. He says she's so smart she can imagine a stick with only one end. Not that my dad's stupid, he must be quite smart to make up a thing like that, but he doesn't take time to think as he's always telling us to do. He's a postman. Sometimes he says he should have stayed in India and become a goldsmith like his father and his grandfather. It makes you feel rich playing with other people's gold, he says, but the gold ran out or something and he had to leave Bombay and come to England and send money back to keep his brothers and sisters.

He's lovely, my dad, though I think I love my nan best. She only came to live with us last year and she still doesn't speak a word of English. She gets along though, goes down to the shops by herself, a little old Indian lady in a *sari*, not even the sort Mum wears, but black or brown because her husband's dead, and tied round in the old fashioned way with the loose flap coming over her shoulder from back to front. She travels by bus and tube all over London, and my brother and I teach her to say 'I'm a senior citizen' instead of 'No English, no speaking' like she does, and to say 'Sorry, I don't speak English so please speak to me in Gujerati or Hindi'. My brother taught her that, though I think it's silly because if she really did go around saying that, they'd think she was daft.

She's only been in London for a year, and she never complains about the cold or anything like that. She says, 'Where my grandchildren are, there I want to be, their faces make the sun shine,' and funny rot like that. She's always telling us stories about when she was a girl in India. We've given her a room on her own, the back room on the first floor of our house in Ealing, just near where the BBC studios are.

Anyway, this story really starts with a song. No, it starts with this boy in school – I might as well be frank since I'm writing this down, and I don't care if Dad or Mum gets to see it. The boy's name is Ralph and his dad's an actor. If you've seen the play *Canterbury Tales* in the West End, or on telly, then you've seen his dad, because he's in it. Ralph's very sweet. I'm the only Indian girl in our class at school, and even though all of them are very friendly, Ralph is the only boy who ever talks to me seriously. He once asked me if I was going to get married to an Indian boy, somebody my dad chose for me. I said maybe I will, but that the ideas in my family are changing, that we are really not super-stitious or anything like that.

'Why does your dad get so jumpy every time I come round? He puts on a face like I was going to rape you or something.'

Until about two weeks ago he used to be going with this girl called Andre. She's also in our class at Gold-hawk Comprehensive. (The boys always call it Colditz Comprehensive.) Andre was his girl, but he used to still sit next to me in class and make her jealous and behave as though he didn't notice that she was staring. If the teachers don't have enough texts and we're sharing books, he always gets one between us and touches my hand when he turns the pages. She's always watching, Andre, but pretending that she's not. He calls me Minihaha because he says I'm small, Indian and funny.

Ralph's going to be an actor. He always gets the highest marks in English and takes over the drama class whenever he's feeling like it. He's clever. He can play the guitar and I think he tries to look like a pop star, with shaded glasses and a sort of smart haircut, long at the back and short on top. He brings the best records to school, not all that reggae rubbish and Donny Osmond and Slade. He listens to David Bowie and the Rolling Stones and all sorts of new groups that no one's ever heard of. He says he's learning to play the sitar from the lead guitarist of a group he's going to join.

One day, about a week ago, he said he wanted to listen to some Hindi pop and I said my dad's only got film songs and he gets them straight from India so he won't let them out of his sight. 'In that case I'll have to listen to them up your house, won't I?' he said.

To tell you the truth, I was very glad he said that, and I told him I'd tell him when he could come because my dad had to be got in the right mood. If Ralph came too often he'd start getting ideas and making a fuss.

I talk to my nan about my friends, so I told her about Ralph and she asked if he was from a good family and whether I liked him. I said that I did like him a little, and there weren't any good or bad families in Britain, they were all the same. She said that that could never be, there was always a difference between gold and lead and the older you get the better you could tell.

My dad has the same sort of ideas. You can't blame him because he must have got them from her. He lectures us on and on about such things. When we went to pick up Nan from the airport, he was saying he hadn't lost respect for his own dad, even though he was dead. My brother's quite cheeky and he said, 'Neither did Hamlet,' but my dad doesn't understand about Shakespeare so the joke was no good on him.

Dad always says that English people put their parents in old people's homes because they have no shame, but we Indians know how to look after our own. Sometimes when he talks that way I like it, it makes me feel different and also better than the rest, because it's true I suppose, they don't have any old folk's homes in India. But there are beggars and hungry people all about the streets and when I point that out my dad says it's true, but what can one do, there are rich and poor everywhere and poor people may be starving but they have good hearts.

'Can't pay the rent with good hearts,' my brother says.

When Dad speaks like this it frightens me too, because I don't really know anything about India. Since I was four I've lived in London and now that I'm fifteen I often think of going to India. My mother always says we're going next year, but Dad says there's not enough money saved and next year never comes. If I start earning my own money I'll save up and go, just for a visit.

The day Ralph came Dad was on the evening shift. Ralph turned up, as always with books and LPs in his hand. We sat in the front room where the record player was and where Mum could have kept an eye on us while she cooked next door in the kitchen. Ralph had been there a few times and he always sat politely, not like at school where he sprawls out on the desks and sits with his trousers pulled to his shins, cross-legged on the cement flower pots in the school playground.

Nan was in the house when he arrived, and Mum had just nipped out to the launderette with two loads. Nan came and sat in the front room with us while we played the discs and talked in English. I kept watching the door for Dad, knowing it wouldn't really matter, if Nan was in the same room. She wanted to know why Ralph wore a necklace – he had a chain and pendant, the sort you buy for a few bob in Shepherds Bush Market. She wanted to know if he was a prince of some sort, or whether he was a dancer. I translated for her and Ralph said that he was the Prince of Darkness, but Nan didn't get the joke and said he was so white, he shouldn't say that about himself.

After we played through some of Dad's LPs, Ralph wanted to put on his own and asked if it was all right. 'There are Indian bells on this one, remind you of the cows tinkling home in the sunset, listen,' he said.

Now I don't listen much to pop, but I was relieved that Dad wouldn't come home to find us playing with his records. So Ralph put on the Stones and we listened. We sat through it and talked. Then he said, 'What about all the old Indian hospitality then, you haven't even offered me a bleeding cup of tea?'

I wished he hadn't said that, because I didn't want to ask Nan to make it and if Mum had been there it would have been all right, but according to Hindu custom you only serve up tea to a young man when your dad has brought him home to look you over as a marriage proposition. I said to Nan that there were cokes in the fridge and she got the hint and perhaps she understood that it was awkward for me so she went and got them herself, and she did a very sweet thing, she brought them on a tray with a can-opener. Ralph said it was a good idea and began to open the can with the can-opener and I split myself laughing because Nan didn't understand what she'd done wrong. She began talking to Ralph in Gujerati as though he understood every word and he just smiled at her.

'Hey, listen to this one,' Ralph said as one song came to an end and another started. 'Are you sure your nan doesn't understand English?'

I didn't know it was going to be a rude song. Personally, I don't think there's anything rude about that song or any other. It's about this girl who likes going out with pop stars and film stars, and I think girls dream about that, at least lots of them in our school do, but this song puts it in a slightly different way. I might as well be frank and say what the song actually says. The words are something about 'star-fucker, star-fucker, star-fucker, star ...' and about missing her two-tongued kisses and wrapping his legs round her thigh, and making her scream all night. We listen to that sort of thing every day in school and there are much worse songs on the radio which have two meanings, like the one about 'my ding-a-ling', which is not really about a bell at all. Even so, I knew that my dad would feel that this was his house and no filth should be brought into it.

I was going to say that to Ralph. I could see from his face that he wanted to see how far he could go with me, he had that sort of defiance, pretending that he was listening to just some old love song. But it was too late. Dad came in taking his grey jacket off, and Ralph said, 'Hello, Mr Desai.'

Dad grunted and he went into the kitchen, asking Nan for the house keys which she kept tied to her *sari*, in a big bunch on her waist. When she first came from India, Dad made a big thing about it and handed them all over to her, saying that she was the boss of the house. He was just going upstairs when he stopped in the doorway and turned round with lines on his brow, crumpled like crushed paper. It was as though someone had said, 'stick 'em up' from behind and he didn't quite understand. He was standing in the door, his body half going out and half coming back, listening to the words that came out of the loudspeakers. I knew he was too shy to say anything in front of Ralph. Still, there was a silence and Nan pushed her way into it, speaking to him about the letters she had to write to India and saying that Mum had the one from her youngest son, Dad's brother, and he could see it when she came back from the launderette. The record was saying something about 'giving it to Steve McQueen' when Dad decided to leave it and went upstairs.

'Can we put something else on?' I asked Ralph. He changed the record and as he looked round at me he grinned slyly, as though he knew that he'd done some mischief and that the thunder behind Dad's frown would soon come crashing down. He finished his can of coke and said he was going straight to his evening job.

'I'll leave the records for you, you can bring them to school tomorrow,' he said.

'Why don't you take them with you? I might forget,' I said. I wanted him to get them out of the house, but I also wanted him to leave them so I could show the others in class that Ralph had been at my house when

I took them back. I felt that he wanted to show them, and Andre, that too.

'No, bring 'em in tomorrow. I can't take them to work, they'll most likely get nicked.'

When Ralph had left I wanted to know what sort of a mood Dad was in so I went up to his room and he was sitting on the bed, still looking angry.

'I'm going to help Mum down the launderette,' I said.

'What kind of boys do you bring into my house?' he asked.

'Oh Dad, don't be so sticky, there aren't any other kind of boys, at least not at our school, and Ralph is best at work, he gets top marks all the time, and you're always telling me to make friends with the top ten.'

Dad didn't reply, he just made a face.

When I came back with loads of washing, the records were still on the player, so I picked them up, intending to take them to the room I shared with Lekha, my sister. I went through the records and found that the Rolling Stones one was missing. I shouted all round the house, but nobody could tell me where it was. I knew that Dad had taken it, so I crawled all round the front room and pretended to be looking for it under the table and behind the couches and under the newspaper. Dad just put on his glasses and began to read the letters my mum gave him, taking not the least bit of notice of me.

I didn't want to start an argument, because I knew he was waiting for me to ask him to give it back and then he'd start on about how English people were different from us, and some words should never pass a girl's lips or ears. I was fed up of telling him that I was Indian but also English, because where you live matters, even more than the blood you have in you, and that my mind was

69

English in a way because I had two sets of ideas, one for the English people I knew and one for the Indians.

When Dad settled down to eat, with Mum fetching him his food, because he ate before all of us, I went up to his bedroom and looked all round. The record wasn't anywhere, but his cupboard was locked. And this is where my nan comes in, and her story, the one she told me.

I saw Ralph in school the next day and told him that I was still listening to his wretched records and my brother wanted to tape them so I'd bring them back later.

'Your old man looked like Geronimo yesterday,' he said. 'I thought hang on, he's gone to the kitchen for his tomahawk.'

'He's funny sometimes,' I said, but I couldn't tell him about the record. It was the same for two days. Ralph would make silly jokes, he'd say I was making record curry and all that. He knew I felt rotten about it.

I went up to Nan's room and sat talking to her that evening. She didn't ask me what was on my mind. I think she knew. So she began telling me her story.

She said that when she was my age in Bombay, which must have been long before the First World War (I can't even *think* that far back except in history lessons), they used to live all together in a big house, nineteen brothers and sisters and cousins and four sets of parents, her own and her uncles and aunts, and her grandad. He must have been my great-great-grandad, and they were all scared of him because he was the chief of the household. He was a kind of tyrant, but he earned the first pay packet in the house, and that made him lord and master. He always wore a turban, and he worked as a goldsmith

70

and she said he was a very good artist and made the most fabulous ear-rings and bangles and things.

One day when the men were all out at work and the boys had gone to school with their slates and chalks (they didn't send girls in those days) the women and girls trooped out of the house to their local market. It was called Grant Road and was spread out under a huge railway bridge near their house. The women had heard that there were all sorts of new things at the market, just off the ship from England and they'd better go fast. Like the sales in Oxford Street, I suppose. She went along with the rest, because she said one thing that girls were taught to do by their mothers and aunts was to bargain with tradesmen and bring the prices down and pretend you weren't going to buy and walk away and come back and keep your face straight to show you didn't really like what they had to sell.

Only the wives of the house, that's Nan's mum and her sisters-in-law, had any money. When they got to the market, there was a huge crowd gathered round a particular street stall. You know what they were selling there? China – English tea-sets and dinner-sets and vases. My nan laughed when she told it. She was remembering the delight with which they looked at these things, because they hadn't seen crockery for home use before. They looked at the coloured patterns and the salesman let them handle the cups and plates. Well, she said, they had seen them before but this was the first time they'd got so close. There was a dinner-set there with a Chinese pattern on it, with bamboo branches and beautiful birds, all red and blue and yellow, in the branches, the same pattern on each plate and dish. They asked the price. They could manage it, they decided, if they pooled their

71

money. Her mum made the decision. Yes, they'd buy them, they'd use all their own money and not touch the housekeeping. When the man wrapped them up in tissue paper and put them in a box, they carried them home like they'd won a trophy in the World Cup or something.

That evening, without telling any of the menfolk, they laid the dinner-set out as a surprise.

'You wouldn't get any like it nowadays,' she said. 'It was all little patterns, carefully done like a silversmith had been working on it.'

They sat down to dinner a little uncertain and very excited. Then the storm broke. Her grandad came in from work and hung up his turban and took off his work shoes and put on his slippers and walked into the dining room, where the women were supposed to serve the meal to the sitting menfolk. His daughters and daughters-in-law watched his face as he saw the china set instead of the silver and brass trays that they normally ate off. They were proud of their display and had even put a table cloth down, 'like the memsahib's house', Nan said.

Her grandad took one look at the Chinese bird crockery and his eyes went blazing mad. He grabbed the table cloth and before their eyes, as they held their breaths, he picked up the lot, took it to the window, and flung it crashing downstairs, two floors down to the courtyard. The crash brought the neighbours to their windows and they caught the last act of the play.

'We are Indians, high caste Indians,' he shouted. 'I won't have this foreign mud in my house, shiny mud that's all it is. Trust women to be fooled by pictures of parrots. I won't eat off shiny mud plates and nobody from my house is going to waste my money on heathen inventions.'

That was the end of that. The women folded their arms before them, and not one of them dared go out to pick up the pieces till he gave the order. The table was set as usual with metal trays in a matter of seconds. Nan said they were always scared of a beating in those days.

'That was sixty years ago, or something,' I said, 'and our dad he still thinks the same. He's thrown away my friend's record, just because he doesn't understand the songs.'

'Sshh, he hasn't thrown it away,' she said, and she giggled like a little girl. 'He was listening to your record when you went to school yesterday, and he locked it up in his cupboard, but I've got the key, so I stole it.'

She pulled the LP out from under her bed.

'What about Dad?' I asked, worried that he'd blame me for going through his cupboards.

'Thieves can't complain about stealing,' she said.

'What happened about the crockery?' I asked her a few days after that. 'Did you ever get to eat off china?'

'Not when my grandad was alive,' she replied. 'It was really different in those days. Men were gods.'

5 KBW

Tahir's gone now. No one to play chess with. I ask my dad for a game and he says he has a union meeting to attend this evening. 'Young Habib would've given you three in a row with one hand tied behind his blooming back,' he says as he goes out.

My dad says they're going to move an Irish family in. He knows that I shall miss Tahir. 'Maybe young Paddy will know some chess,' he says.

Their flat was exactly like ours, except the other way round, like when you see a thing in a mirror. Like twins growing out of each other our two flats were. And I was Tahir's best friend. The windows are still smashed, but the flat's been boarded up, like some others on our estate. It goes for kilometres. You must of heard of it, it's called the Devonmount Estate, Borough of Hackney. I shan't go to cricket practice today. I dropped out after Tahir left. We joined the team together so I think it's only right that we pull out together.

My mother don't understand. She says, 'Go on out and do something. Go and play cricket, you can't help the way the world is. Don't sit there looking like a month of wet Sundays.'

Dad understands. 'Son, you're right. Don't have no truck with racialist swine.' He always talks like that. Mum still needles him about being a Communist and he always replies that he's a Red in her bed, and the day she tries to put him under for his political views, he'll leave. They all know my dad on the estate. Twenty-two years he's been here.

I was born here and went to school here, to Devonmount Juniors and then Devonmount Comprehensive, no less. Tahir came here eight months ago. His dad came from Bangladesh, because they was driven out by the riots. That's what Tahir told me. He came straight into the fourth form. I took him to school the first day. My dad introduced hisself to Mr Habib as soon as they moved in, and he said to me at dinner that day, 'My boy, a Bengali family has moved in next door, and I've told mister that you are going to take master to school. He's in your school and I want you to take him in and stick him outside the Headmaster's office.'

That's how I met Tahir. I asked him what games he liked and he said cricket so I took him to Mr Hadley, the local vicar who runs the cricket team, and Tahir bowled for us. He was great. He lit up when they said they wanted to try him. Mr Hadley gave him the bat and bowled to him, and Tahir struck it hard to mid-off and was caught first go. Then Hadley gave him the ball. Tahir stroked it like it was a pigeon or something and when he looked up there was a shine in his eyes, same as you get out of the toe of a shoe when you put spit on the leather. He took a short run and bowled that ball. It spun at an amazing speed to leg-side.

'What do we have here?' Mr Hadley said, and his glasses gleamed. Tahir was our best spin bowler. He took four wickets in the match against the Mercer's Estate. When we won that match we were sure to get to the finals with the Atlanta Atlases. They were the best estate club going. If we beat them we'd be champs of Hackney. If you don't live in Hackney and don't live on the Devonmount, you don't know what that means. But I'll tell you what it means. It means Vietnam, North Vietnam that is, beating America in a war. That's what it means, a little country with a lot of determination, and without two ha'pennies to rub together, beating what my dad calls the biggest military machine ever built by man or money. Because ours is the worst estate. The flats are filthy and the stairs and the courtyard are never cleaned. There's coal dumps in the yards and half the places are boarded up. You should have seen the Habib's flat. Water pouring down the wall of one bedroom, the wallpaper all peeling off like scabs, and the roof-plaster all torn to bits. My dad said that it was nothing less than a crying shame for a workers' government to treat the workers so. My mum said she remembered when she was a little girl, and they ought to be thankful for a bathful of water which was hot.

The door of their flat has been forced open and the young ones play in there. That's what they call kids who still go to primary school on the Devonmount. I'm not a little 'un any more, I'm twelve and I'm not interested in climbing the garbage carts and pulling bits off people's cars and playing cowboys and Indians or hide and seek or cops and robbers in the empty flats. I used to be, and in those days I couldn't see why everyone on the estate complained about it. To me the empty flats were space. They gave you the feeling not that you belonged there, but that the place belonged to you so you could never leave it. Last year they built an adventure playground for the little 'uns on an empty site, and they went in hordes there, but after a while they didn't like it, they stopped going and started back in the empty flats again. There was nothing to nick in the adventure playground but the empties. You can find and flog all sorts of things around here. There are some blokes on the estate who'll give you quite a few pence for a load of pipes or even for boards and doorknobs and toilet seats and that, and the kids on the estate break in and rip everything up. It's only when a flat has been completely ripped up that it becomes a place to play in. It gets cleaned out like a corpse gutted by sharks. I walked through their flat yesterday and it's been done over.

When Tahir's family first moved in, the people around didn't like it. They didn't go to the trouble to worry them, but the boys from C Block came to our building and painted 'Niggers Out' on the landing. My dad said it was a shame and he gave me some turps and a rag and asked me to clean it off, but I couldn't, it wouldn't come off. He said it was an insult to coloureds, and I know it was because the lads from C Block don't like coloured people – they're always picking on Pakis and coons when they're in a gang. My mum says they only do it because they're really scared of them, but I don't think they are. When Tahir and I came home from school together they used to shout, 'Want to buy an elephant?' and all that bollocks. Tahir never took any notice. He always walked looking straight ahead, but even though he didn't understand what they were saying, he'd become very silent and not say a word to me all the rest of the way. I still think I was his best friend. There was always six of them and they was bigger than us. Sometimes they'd even come to our block and shout from downstairs. If Tahir's father heard them he'd come out on the gallery and shout back at them. I think he was a very brave man. He wasn't scared of anyone and he'd say, 'Get out, swine,' because those were the only swear words in English that he knew. He didn't speak English very much and when my dad met him on the stairs or invited him round for a cup of tea, he'd just say, 'It is very kind, don't trouble, please don't trouble.' Tahir told me once that his father was a karate expert and could break three bricks with one hand. And he was strong. One day when I was in their flat, he lifted a whole big refrigerator all by hisself from the bottom of the stairs.

The trouble all started with the newspapers. There was a story in the *Sun* one day which said that two people in London had died of typhoid. My mum and dad talked about it at home and Mrs Biggles, my mum's mate, said that a girl in C Block had been taken to St Margaret's Hospital and was under observation there. The girl was called Jenny and we knew her 'cause she used to go to the same school as my little sister Lynn.

The story went around the estate that there was typhus in the East End, and everybody was talking about it. Then a funny thing happened. We play cricket down in Haggerston Park and after the game, when Mr Hadley has locked the kit away in the hut at the corner, he takes us all to the vicarage and he gives us bags of crisps and cups of cocoa, and lets us listen to his records. Well, this last Saturday, we had a lot of kids turn up for cricket practice. Usually there's only the team, about thirteen lads, but this time there was eighteen because Mr Hadley said we had to have proper trials for the juniors team. We all sat around while James and Mr Hadley made the cocoa. He peeped around the door and said, 'There's only seven mugs, so you'll have to share the cocoa.'

We said, 'Right ho, umpire,' because that's what he likes to be called. Sometimes he tells us, if he's feeling like talking about church, that vicars are umpires from God and that life is like a test match between good and evil. I think Mr Hadley explains things well, but I still don't believe in it. My dad says that Hadley should stick to cricket and not brainwash the team, because my dad's dead against the Christians. He's an atheist but our mum tells us not to take any notice of him, because she believes in God.

Anyway, on this Saturday, James brought in the cups of cocoa to the team and gave them to every second person, as two people had to share. We were sitting in a circle on the carpet and Nick was changing the records. Every now and then someone would get up and there'd be an argument about whether to have David Essex or the Slade on next. Tahir never said a word. He was holding his steaming cup of cocoa and you could see the gaps in his teeth when he smiled. The lads would ask him to whistle and he'd always try but he couldn't do it on account of the big gap in his front teeth.

Next to Tahir there was a boy called Alan, and when Tahir had taken a few sips of the cocoa after it had cooled, he passed it on to him. The rest of us were fighting for the mugs, just mucking about sort of, and eating crisps at the same time. I was watching this boy Alan, who had freckles and a thin face which looked scared most of the time, and I could see that he didn't want to take the cup from Tahir.

'Have it, I've finished,' Tahir said.

Alan said he didn't want any cocoa, so Tahir turned

79

to try and give the mug back to James.

'Everyone's got one,' James said. 'They're sharing if they haven't.'

'You didn't get,' Tahir said, smiling upward at James.

'I'll share someone's,' James replied, but when Tahir tried to give him his cup, he said, 'No, that's all right, you have the rest, I'll get some later.'

Tahir put his cup down in the middle of the carpet. All the cocoa from the other mugs was finished, but no one wanted to pick up Tahir's mug. Then it struck me. Mr Hadley shouted from the kitchen that the milk was finished, and there was a sort of silence in the room.

Tahir was searching the other faces. 'Anybody could drink it,' he said.

Nobody picked up the mug. It stood on the carpet, not even half drunk. I looked at the others. A second before they'd been laughing and talking, but now there was only the sound of the record player. I think Tahir understood. I looked at Alan. He had a look on his face like a dog that's been whipped. The others were looking at him too.

'I don't want any,' he said.

Mr Hadley, his red face shining still with the sweat of the game, came in and said that it had been a damned hard selection and if we put in a bit of practice we could beat the Atlases. 'Fine cricket,' he said, and he rubbed his hands as usual. 'With fine weather it'll be finer.'

Tahir was silent on the way home. He kept looking at his feet as we walked, and he looked thinner and even smaller than he normally looked.

When I got home, Mrs Biggles was there in the kitchen. 'They suspect typhus, the girl's shaking with fever and the poor dear didn't even recognise her own mother,' she was saying. She was asking Lynn questions about the girl Jenny who was in hospital. 'It's not known here,' the doctor said to her mother, 'it's the foreigners have brought it in, that's for sure, from Istanbul and Pakistan and now from that Ugandan Asians' place. We've never had these things here,' he went on.

'It's the blacks bring these things in here ...' she said.

My mum went dead silent. After Mrs Biggles had left, my dad put his mug of tea on the table and said he didn't want Mrs Biggles and her filthy mouth in his house, but Mum pretended she didn't hear and kept looking at the telly screen.

Another odd thing happened, on the following Monday. I woke up and dressed for school. Usually by the time my cornflakes are on the table, Dad's gone to work, but I found him in the kitchen that morning. He looked worried. He was sitting at the kitchen table with his hair brushed back and shiny with hair oil. He was talking to Mum, and then he took his coat and left. Mum said the people on the estate were rats and they needed poisoning, or leastways they deserved it. 'He took him to the pub once,' she said, 'just once as far as I know.'

'Who?' I asked.

'That Mr Habib from next door, your Tahir's father, even though the poor man couldn't drink on account of his religion, he had to drag him along just to show everyone.'

'Who took him?'

'Them people from C,' she said, 'they've painted things on our door. I wish Dad would call the police.'

As I walked out to school I turned to the door and it said 'K B W' in big black letters.

Dad was furious with Mum for telling me about it, and they had a right row that evening. Mum had scrubbed it off the door with sandpaper.

'Did you come back with Tahir?' she asked.

Tahir had been at school that day, but he behaved a bit strange. He wasn't there for the last lesson and I reckoned he must have hopped it.

'What does it mean?' I asked my dad, remembering the letters.

'It means your dad is poking his nose into other people's business,' my mum said.

'You know what they painted on our door, son?' my dad asked.

'I saw it,' I said.

'It means Keep Britain White,' Dad said. He looked grey in the face and serious. You know what that means, son. It used to be the Jews in the thirties, now it's bleedin' Indians and Pakistanis. Some people have seen you with Tahir.'

'More like they've seen you chatting like old friends to Habash, or whatever his name is,' Mum said.

'I've seen a lot of it and I hoped you wouldn't grow up in a world with these anti-working-class prejudices. I don't care what your mum says, but we've got to fight it. I've been fighting it, and I hope my son and grandson will fight it too.'

'And a lot of good it's done you,' Mum said.

But I was kind of proud of my dad.

'They are fascist scum, lad,' he said. He always calls me 'lad' when he gets to lecturing about his politics.

'Don't go putting your ideas into the boy's head,

you leave him to think as he pleases.'

Dad ignored her. He sat with his palms on his knees and with his tall back pushed against the chair, the way he always did when he thought he was teaching me the facts of life.

'You know this typhoid, lad,' he said. 'People are blaming the Habibs for bringing it in. But any law court in this country knows they're innocent. It's ignorance and superstition. This girl Jenny went to Spain on the school trip with our Lynn, didn't she?' This was said more to Mum than to me.

I hardly slept at all that night. The next day the papers said that the girl Jenny was worse and that several cases of typhoid had been found and more people had been put under observation in the East End hospitals. I was thinking that I knew why the cricket team hadn't wanted to touch Tahir's cocoa. I was wishing I had picked it up. I knew that Tahir must be thinking the same thing too. It struck me that he must have thought that I had the same idea as the rest of them.

Sometimes I have funny dreams and that's when I can't sleep. That night I dreamt of the letters K B W painted up across our door, and then the letters spread out with other letters on to the whole of the estate, and the letters growing and becoming bigger and bigger till they were too heavy and had to come crashing down, falling on top of me, the K like two great legs and the W spinning round like giant compasses.

I went very tired to school. I didn't tell Mum about the dream. Tahir wasn't in the playground and he wasn't at registration. I thought he might be late, but he never came late, and then it struck me that I knew he wouldn't come to school that day.

I stayed in that night and so did Dad. He usually goes down the pub for a jar, but he didn't bother that night. He turned on the telly and I could see from the way he folded his legs, and from his eyes which were glued on the screen but not taking in the programme, that he was worried. He usually starts on at Lynn when he's like that, asks her to polish her shoes for school the next day and for her homework and everything. It felt to me too as though something was about to happen, and it did.

I heard the crash and then another thud and another crash of glass and a woman screaming. It was Tahir's mother. Dad sprang up from his chair. I felt that he had been expecting it. He rushed to the door. Mum came out of the kitchen. The crash of brick or stone sounded as though it was in our own house. Dad opened the door and went out on to the gallery.

'Bastard, cowards!' I heard. It was Mr Habib shouting his lungs out.

Dad rushed back into the flat. 'There's twenty of them out there.'

'Shall I call the police?' Mum asked.

Dad didn't answer. Everyone hates coppers on our estate, and no one ever calls them. Coppers don't need invitations. I could hear the blokes downstairs shouting. Mum pushed Lynn away from her and went out on to the gallery.

Mr Habib was still shouting, 'You are all bastards, white bastards.'

Then we heard the running steps on the stairs. The blokes were coming up, and they were shouting too: 'Paki filth,' and, 'The girl's dead.'

It was all hell. Mr Habib went in and got Tahir's

84

cricket bat. The blokes from C Block had bottles. There was more crashing of glass and Mrs Habib kept screaming things in Indian and I could hear Tahir crying and shouting and a lot of thumping.

'Why don't you help him?' my mum shouted to Dad. 'What kind of bloody Communist are you?' But Dad was pushing her into the kitchen.

'Shut your mouth,' he said to her. He never talks like that normally, but he looked as though he'd pissed himself. 'Let the police handle this. There's twenty of them out there.'

By the time the police came, with sirens blaring, pulling into the courtyard, jumping out and slamming their car doors, the blokes were gone.

I said, 'Mum I'm going out,' and before she could stop me I went to the door and unbolted it. Other people had come out of their flats. The galleries of all the floors were now full of people trying to see what had happened. The police called an ambulance, and they took Mr Habib, who was lying outside his door groaning, to hospital. Tahir was bending over him when the coppers came with an Indian bloke and started asking questions. Tahir looked up at me as I stepped out, and he looked away. His dad had all blood streaming down his face. The day after, the blood marks were still there, all over the gallery.

Two hours later, we were all still awake. It was still as death outside and silent.

'I'll take it up with the council,' my dad said. I knew what he felt. He had wanted to help Tahir's dad, I am sure, but he felt helpless. There were too many of the others, he couldn't have said nothing.

'I wouldn't be seen dead at that girl's funeral,' Dad said after a while.

Four Indian blokes came and took Tahir and his mum and all their stuff away that same night and we could hear the coppers who'd stayed behind arguing with them.

The next day at cricket Mr Hadley asked me where Tahir was. The other boys told him the whole story, that bricks had been thrown through their windows and that Tahir's dad was in hospital.

Mr Hadley knew our school and he turned up there the next day. The Headmaster sent for Tahir and for me from class and we walked together to the office without a word. Mr Hadley was there. He said he was sorry to hear that Tahir's family had been in an unfortunate incident and that he wanted Tahir to come to cricket practice.

Tahir answered all his questions about where they were living and that. He said, 'Yes, sir,' when Mr Hadley said that he must realise that he had a lot of good friends like me and that wherever he lived he must continue to play for Devonmount. He said, 'Yes, sir,' his legs apart, his hands folded behind his back, his head bent and his lips tight together, his eyes moving from Mr Hadley's face to the floor. But he never came again.

6 Good at Art

Raju was shy. He didn't say much and he hadn't any real friends amongst the other sixth formers. He couldn't play cards, didn't like ping pong, wasn't interested in the Velvet Underground or in David Bowie or any of the other crazes that periodically captured the rest of them. He couldn't even tell jokes about Irishmen and though he listened carefully, he could rarely understand them.

His usual place was in an armchair in the corner of the sixth form room, behind a copy of the *Daily Mirror* or the *Sun*, away from the radio and the record player which blared at the gossiping, coffee-drinking cardplaying groups. So when Kim brought the new art teacher round the room and introduced him, as the Deputy Head had told her to do, she made it a point to take him to Raju's corner.

'That's Raju, he's nervous, but he's the best artist of this lot.'

The man with her smiled and said he had a right to be nervous in a mad house, and he put his hands over his ears. He was conscious that the group around the record player was sizing him up and at the same time was determined not to show any extra politeness because he was new.

'What's the matter, don't you like Genesis?' one of the boys asked over the din.

'Genesis?' he said. 'It sounds like apocalypse,' but they didn't get his joke.

'Take no notice of them. They behave so childishly, some of the time,' Kim said, a mock annoyance on her face.

When they'd gone, Raju retreated behind his paper again. He'd been taken by surprise by the new art teacher. They'd been expecting him to turn up for a week to replace Mr Cole, who'd had a heart attack.

'Cole's blacked out,' Steve had said. The Headmaster had told them that the new art teacher was a very talented and qualified young man.

'Seen the new art geezer?' Lesley asked that morning.

'You mean ...'

'Yeah, the Paki bloke we saw with Dunny down the hall, real freak.'

'If he's so talented and all, what's he want to come to a dump like this?'

'Because he's a Paki, and it's better than trying to get bus fares out of you.' Steve said.

'Paki-Picasso,' Lesley said.

'Very good, want to paint an elephant?' one of the others said, mimicking an Indian accent.

'He's got more A levels and degrees, and that, than you've had hot dinners,' Kim said.

'Hope he speaks English better'n my doctor.'

'The way Dunny was saying his name I thought he was Irish,' Steve said.

'That's the way she was pronouncing it. It's a very common Indian name,' Raju said, thinking that he could offer something to the conversation.

'Like Andy-Gandhy,' Lesley said.

'Oh do leave off,' Kim said, the edge of irritation in

her voice telling Raju that she felt protective towards him.

Raju didn't feel he needed her protection, but was glad of it anyway. She had been, in a sense, his guardian angel in the sixth form. If the sixth were planning anything or if there was a conversation in which everybody joined, it would be Kim who, with some remark, would invite Raju to join in. She was in the upper sixth and he was in the lower.

Raju felt she was the most mature of the lot, even though she was younger than they. Raju had bothered to look up her birthday in the register when one of the teachers asked him to return it to the office.

Of course she wasn't to know that part of the reason Raju had wanted to stay on at school and not go into partnership with his uncle in the grocery business, as his father had insisted, was her. She wouldn't know that he had daydreams about her, and that when she singled him out to say something polite, he felt a thrill, a strange ticklish feeling which he was shy of calling love.

The teachers all liked Raju. He never said a rude word to anybody, and he was considered very good at art. He spent most of his free periods in the art room, drawing and sketching the models, the broken violin, the bottles and pots and table lamps, the oranges and apples that Mr Cole had left around the dark, bare room. He told himself that he would try for the A level, and the Deputy Head told him that he would have to wait for the new teacher to arrive and decide.

When Ravi, for that was the art teacher's name, arrived and looked through their folders of work he said, 'Good God, you'll never make A level with this rubbish.

Haven't you done anything apart from these shady objects?'

'We've done lots of painting,' Raju said. 'They're behind the lockers.'

Ravi looked at the paintings, all on cardboard and sugar paper, and he bit his lower lip, and smoothed his hair self-consciously. 'Look, you can't all be landscape freaks,' he said. 'How did you land up all doing the same things? Mind you I like most of them, but they look like you did them from slides or something.'

'We did,' Kim said. 'Mr Cole believed in bringing the outside world into school.'

Ravi got down to hard work with that group. They hated him at first. They thought he was too cocky, too flash in his dress, too familiar with them. 'At least he believes in getting us the bloody A level. Old King Cole didn't have a clue,' one of the boys said.

As their folders began to swell with work and their heads with Ravi's careful praise, the group decided that they could cooperate with him.

Raju wasn't sure. Mr Cole had always dealt with kids as they should be dealt with, Raju thought. At first he even resented the fact that Ravi brought in a hundred new ideas and spent the evenings of his first week painting the walls of the art room. Mr Cole never stayed beyond bell time. His little joke was, 'If you want me, my phone number is RUShome 345,' and Raju was disturbed by the clatter of the machines and furnaces and potters' wheels that Ravi began to install, inviting the group to help him with them after school.

Raju felt that Ravi knew of this resentment but had decided to ignore it. He had thrown himself wholeheartedly into shaking their sleepy art department into a busy awakening.

Besides, Raju felt that Ravi's slightly West Indian accent was phoney and forced and cheeky for an Indian. He had to admit, nevertheless, that Ravi had some warmth, he'd talk to you as an equal and let you call him by his first name even though Raju never did. Old Cole was always telling him that these new-fangled art teachers didn't know about art and didn't know about kids and didn't know about teaching. 'They're all lay-abouts and Communists, and the Head and the Governors are stacking the pack with them. Something under-hand is afoot,' he would say and chuckle at his own joke.

Raju had been Mr Cole's favourite and still felt loyal to him. He was the only one out of his group who had sent him a 'get well soon' card in hospital, until the Deputy Head had told the rest of the sixth formers, and they agreed with her, that Raju's thoughtfulness had put them to shame.

'Let's paint him one,' Steve suggested, sorry to have been reminded of their collective ingratitude.

Ravi helped plan the card. It was to be a collage of Mr Cole's face stuck on to the bodies of Superman, Batman, a Dalek and others, doing amazing feats of strength. Lesley and Steve got down to drawing the card, but when they got to drawing the heads they couldn't get the features right. They asked Ravi to do the heads, but he said he'd never seen what their wonderful Mr Cole looked like.

'Oh, you know, a sort of turnip head and a long neck and ears like Mr Spock.'

'Right. Try and imagine the Loch Ness monster in a tweed jacket and bags.'

'Don't be so mean,' Kim protested, 'and anyway get on with the card.'

'Can't do the blinkin' head.'

'Then let Raju do it,' Kim suggested.

'Come on, Leonardo,' Steve said.

'He's t'riffic on heads,' one of the others said.

Raju had in fact been waiting for the invitation. He was at his own work a little away from the group which had gathered around Lesley's desk. They made way for him and crowded round as he took the stool Lesley had vacated and began to erase the faint sketchings of malformed heads above the muscular action that Steve and Lesley had begun to colour. 'I can only do it in pencil,' Raju said.

They watched as Raju, with small strokes, as though he were writing a script, brought the face of Mr Cole from out of the sheet like a face emerging from a mist. He shaded the hollows of the cheeks. In the pupils of the eyes he captured with a shiver of highlight the inspired madness that seemed to leap out of his subject's forehead.

'You got him, spot on. Great,' Lesley said.

'Colour it in now,' Steve said.

'No. Leave it in pencil,' Ravi said, 'you can't paint over drawings.'

There were five heads in all to do, and as Raju worked, cosy in the admiration of the group, he thought of Mr Cole in his hospital bed. On the one hand he felt excited that the old man would recognise part of it as his work, and on the other hand he had an uneasy feeling that Mr Cole would hate the card. It wasn't the sort of thing he would have encouraged them to do. The card was one way of telling Mr Cole that they were happy and busy without him, that 'art' at the school had changed, that his years of broken violins and fractured pots had been swept away with the cobwebs. The rest of them couldn't have thought of that, they were just being nice, and they were also playing up to Ravi, using the styles and the freedom he'd shown them. A flush of shame at his unintended disloyalty came over Raju. He thought for a moment that he shouldn't have participated in this card lark. He shouldn't have let himself be flattered into doing the heads. But his pencil wouldn't stop. He had no words with which to say what he felt to the others, they wouldn't understand. He knew that the rest of them treated him as though he was Cole's pet and he wanted to outlive that reputation.

While Raju worked at the card Ravi made up an envelope for it.

'It won't fit in a post-box, and we can't really fold it.' Steve observed.

'Go and deliver it yourself,' Ravi answered, as they passed the finished card round for signatures.

'Come on, Raju, put your handle there,' Lesley said, handing him the pen.

'I've already sent one,' Raju said. He had decided that at least he wasn't going to sign the card with the rest of them. Cole would notice that.

'It isn't a cheque.'

'I think one is enough,' Raju said, determined to be firm.

'Suit yourself, mate,' Lesley said, shrugging.

'I'd feel silly sending two cards to the same person. They'd think you're in love with them or something.'

93

'Can we go with it in school-time?' Steve asked Ravi.

'I don't see why not,' Ravi said, 'you can say I let you out.' They were jubilant.

'Straight up?'

'We'll be back for lunch.'

'Sure, go on,' Ravi said, 'I've got to get this wheel set up. Not much I can do with you.'

They were gone and Raju dipped his head into his work. He didn't acknowledge Ravi's presence.

'Have you ever done a portrait in oils?' Ravi asked after a while.

Raju shook his head.

'Why don't you try it? Not straight on canvas, but after you mess around a bit I can stretch the skins for you.'

Raju was quite excited with the idea, but he didn't want Ravi to know that. He just lifted his head to say yes, he'd try it after he'd finished what he was doing.

'How long have you been in Britain?' Ravi asked.

'Since I was eight.'

'And your parents, where do they come from?'

'India.'

'Yes I know, but it's a big place as you'll remember.'

'From Jullunder.'

'Never been there. You know I'm from Bombay.'

Raju didn't acknowledge the remark.

'Have you ever been back to India?'

Raju shook his head.

'I can't go back there, though I'd like to. Get away from London and the cold.'

'Why can't you go back?' Raju asked, his interest faintly aroused.

'Oh, all sorts of things. Running away from it, you know, women and politics and so on. I got involved with an anti-Government movement. I used to teach at the University, and they put a couple of my friends in jail.'

'Are you a Communist?'

'Yes, I am, sort of, but it's very complicated. Do you know anything about Indian politics?'

'My father gets the newspaper. He knows everything, but I don't bother. Still, I'm very interested, my uncle was a Communist.'

'I suppose you feel quite British. You've decided to stay in England?'

Raju hadn't decided anything. That sort of question hadn't crossed his mind. 'I want to do art. Can you do art in India?' For a year or two now he'd made up his mind that he'd be an art teacher, like Mr Cole, but it hadn't struck him that it would mean giving up the possibility of working in India.

'You can do lots of art in India, but you have to do a bit of fighting too.'

As the weeks passed Ravi became the group's favourite teacher. Raju found that Ravi was constantly telling him things about India and the college where he used to teach, and forcing him to think about things he hadn't considered before. Ravi showed him how to work on metal and make bangles and bands out of wire and out of copper plates. Slowly his ambition shifted from wanting to be like Mr Cole, to wanting to be at least a bit like Ravi. He talked about his new teacher at home, and brought Ravi's arguments and sayings back to try them on his dad. At school he spent more and more time in the art room and found that he wasn't alone, that the rest of the sixth form had taken up the gadgets in the art room as their latest craze. Steve was always there, and Lesley and Kim.

While they worked, they talked to Ravi. He'd go down to the pub with them at lunch and play darts with the boys and he'd give them lifts home in his van after school. When some teachers in the staff room complained that he was getting too familiar with the sixth formers, Ravi came down and told them about the row he'd had.

'He can talk,' Lesley said, referring to a senior member of staff, 'the second year's call him Pinching Tom, he's always up the girls' skirts.'

'Bent,' Steve said, 'a cross between Hitler and Danny La Rue.'

Raju found himself drawn into the class circle. He began to say things, and at first the rest of them were amazed. He even bought himself a pair of jeans and an embroidered denim shirt because he had overheard Kim talking to another girl about them, and he stopped wearing school uniform as the rest of them had done a year before.

Everyone in the sixth knew who fancied whom. Some of the boys and girls paired off and went out with each other and acquired reputations for being loose, or for being tight, or for being nice or flash or over-sexed. Raju heard it all and was glad in a way that he had nothing to do with it. And yet he longed to have the confidence to ask a girl out. There were all sorts of things that stopped him. He would have to keep it a secret from his parents, who wouldn't approve. Still, that wasn't what kept him from trying. He had the feeling that he wasn't capable of it. He had no words with which to approach a girl. He knew the games the rest of them played, or at least he thought he could imagine them, because in spite of all the pairing off that went on, you could never actually hear the boys asking the important question. That seemed to go on in secret. Or maybe nobody asked, they just understood that they were in love, Raju thought.

He longed to be able to steer Kim round to a conversation about a film, or about records, and wait for a sign from her, test her out. If the sign came and the way was clear, he could ask her if she wanted to meet that evening at the Elephant and go to the pictures. Or he could get her phone number after talking to her and phone her in the evening to continue the conversation and ask her then. That way he wouldn't have to ask face to face and if she said 'no', he could pretend it never happened.

So Raju's secret passion stayed a secret, but it grew. He watched Kim with an uncanny interest. When they were left alone in the art room, even for a moment while Ravi went to the stock cupboard or something, a strange feeling came over him, a sort of thrill in the chest. She would talk to him about the work they were doing. She began to work very hard at art towards the end of the term, and he overheard the boys saying that there was something wrong with her, she'd turned weird with overwork and over-enthusiasm.

Raju didn't think there was anything wrong with her. He felt, but hardly admitted even to himself, that her work was in some way connected with him, that she stayed behind in the art room day after day because of him. He felt she was returning his attention and she began asking him strange questions, about whether he remembered India.

'I've only heard of Delhi and Bombay, but you're not from there, are you, Raju?'

'I'm from Camberwell,' he said, smiling.

'I wish I wasn't. They're such a pig-headed lot.'

She would ask him to criticise her work and Raju discovered a new language in himself. He began to talk about pictures and design. Ravi would join in and usually take over the conversation, bringing out prints and art books to show them the work of strange artists like Escher and Dadd and Kitaj.

Raju felt that Kim was the first person in school who wanted to know what he was like before and after the starting and finishing buzzer of the school day. 'Do you eat Indian food at home?' she once asked, and she inquired about his family, his mother, and what language they spoke at home and even about him getting married.

'Will you let your mum choose your wife, then?'

'No chance,' Raju said. 'This is England and my parents can't bully me about. My cousin ran away and married whoever he wanted. An Irish girl.'

He saw her smile at this. He loved the way her broad mouth opened into a narrow smile, her one buck tooth flashing the mischief in her face. He thought he'd managed to tell her indirectly, ever so indirectly, that his thoughts about girls and about getting married had something to do with her. And she had smiled. He thought of her expression ten times in the next few days, and he wished that Ravi hadn't come in and interrupted their conversation.

Kim seemed quite willing to carry it on later.

'Ask your mum, please, how to cook a real Indian

curry and tell me about it, would you do that for me?'
she asked, and Raju thought if she only knew how
willing he'd be to do anything for her. Get her the
recipe? He'd get her the Golden Fleece if she asked for it.

He spent that evening pestering his mother for a
recipe and writing it out for Kim, changing 'ghee' to
'margarine' and making a trip to his uncle's grocery
shop to ask him what the English names for 'dhania'
and 'jeera' were.

'I'm going to try it tonight or tomorrow,' Kim said
when he gave her the neat sheet of paper.

For the next few days Raju waited for a sign from
her. He was certain that she wanted to pass some mess-
age to him, some mysterious token. She was telling him,
by the way she looked at him, that she understood the
transparent silence that he'd wrapped himself in. She
had put a value on his shyness and wasn't going to
crash through it, but she was going to ask him, in careful steps, for access through that armour. He saw himself, in a daydream, walking down a long street and
she coming towards him and taking his hand, hesitantly,
and turning and walking with him and getting him to
talk as he had never talked before, explaining how his
silence and his modesty were a cover for a feeling as
deep as a well.

She would also understand that he had respect for
girls, and being Indian, he wouldn't expect to kiss her
and feel her and fondle her just because she had agreed
to walk down the street with him. She would give herself willingly to him and he would only take what was
given. But he knew that nothing would be given without
asking.

Two days after Kim took the recipe from him, they

were working together in the art room. Kim asked him which way he was walking home, and he looked into her face to reply and felt his tongue thicken with excitement and his words coming out in a jumble. He packed his stuff and they left together.

Ravi had gone home early so they shut the art room behind them and walked together to Oval tube station. When she left him, she didn't say 'See yuh', she said, 'Goodnight Raju, you'll be in school early tomorrow as always, won't you?'

Raju felt that the blue of her eyes had suddenly turned to silver, and in that mirror was reflected the map of his hopes and maybe of hers. Even though there was some satisfaction in that, he felt his courage had failed him. As they walked together, his folder of drawings under his arm, and her skirt swinging very carefully around her hips, he had made the effort to turn the conversation to a subject which would enable him to ask her what she did with her evenings.

'I want to try some oil portraits,' he said, 'but I'll need a model, you know, who'll sit without fidgeting right through.'

'Oh, can I have my picture taken please?' she said. 'I'd love to do it for you, but I suppose I can't, because I can't really keep still.'

'I'll make a film instead, then,' Raju said.

'Why don't you ask Ravi? He gets paid to teach you doesn't he? He'll be a good model, with all that thick black hair and funny browny-greeny eyes.'

'No, he won't do.'

'Not your sort, huh? Not handsome enough for you.'

'Not that, he has too much work.'

'Him? He's a lazy sod,' Kim said, looking up quickly at Raju's face and looking away.

'I must practise portraits for A level,' Raju said.

'You'll easy make it and go to art school. Ravi says he thinks you'll be a great illustrator.'

Raju was flattered. He scanned her face and distinctly saw in it something unexpected. She was shy too, she wanted to make some move, to tell him something, but she too found herself incapable.

The next day at school he started on his project. He asked Ravi for a canvas and began sketching a face in pencil. He didn't tell Ravi what he was working at, and he waited till Kim came into the room and looked at her face in a new way. His eyes were not watching, but measuring. He was looking at the pores of her skin, the pinkness, so patchy and running into light, even yellowish skin, her eyes separated by a stubby bridge. He was looking for every twist and shadow of this face that he'd looked at so many times before, and he felt that he was beginning to know it afresh, to know it like an object, coolly.

As soon as he felt that the picture he was working on was faintly identifiable, he took it home. When the sketch was finished, he turned the canvas over and began the portrait in oils. He propped it up against the wall of his room and knelt before it to work on it every day after school. Working for hours on one little piece of Kim's face, and working from his sketch and from his memory, he felt a possessiveness begin to come over him. Slowly, brush stroke by brush stroke, he was bringing her into his room.

Then it was finished, the schoolgirl face which seemed to say that it knew more about life's uncertainties than a schoolgirl should know. When it was done he felt a bit exhausted, and possessive of it more than proud. He had struggled with the hundreds of images and expressions that he could imagine when he thought of her, to distil just one, the one that had all the others in it. When he took it to school, he had a plan. He'd take the first opportunity to ask her out, and he'd give her the canvas. He would return the little piece of possessiveness he had earned; he would give it back to her.

Ravi was the first to see the canvas. 'So that's what you've been doing, you sly bugger,' he said, and then, 'Raju, it's really beautiful. You've caught her as she is, half old lady and half Lolita. Listen, baby, it's fantastic.'

He held the portrait and looked at it in the light. Then he placed it against the blackboard and ran, taking the steps two at a time, to call the rest of the sixth to see it.

Raju's heart sank as he heard them approaching down the corridor. He felt suddenly naked. That canvas was a confession. They would all know, they would take the piss out of him. For an instant he felt like grabbing the canvas and running out with it, or even tearing it up. But a pride in his work, and the knowledge that he'd done something truthful and had spoken openly for the first time, kept him sitting where he was.

They came straight to the canvas. The sight of it struck them as they walked in. Kim was at the back of the crowd. Without a word they let her follow her fixed stare to the front.

'Should've been down to here, in 3D,' Steve said, indicating with his hand below the canvas that Raju should have painted her down to the waist. The moment of dumb wonder had passed. They gathered round

Raju and thumped him on his back, as though he'd scored a goal for the school team. Kim stood in front of the painting.

'Raju, it's very good, like a twin,' she said. Raju saw that she was embarrassed. His shyness had flown to her and her boldness to him. He understood, sensing her excitement, that it was not only himself he had exposed in painting her picture.

'I'll show it to the staff room,' Ravi said.

'Not to old Bodger, he'll get over-excited, not good for him.'

'Don't you like it, Kim?' Ravi asked.

'You should have posed in the nude!' Lesley said. 'Blimey, how many hours were you cloistered with our Kim, Raju?'

Of course, something changed in the sixth form from that day. There was evidently a new respect for Raju, both for his skill and for his daring in choosing Kim as a subject. In Kim herself, Raju detected a coolness. She was pulling away from him, as if she feared, ever so slightly, that Raju had declared with that picture that he wanted to work some spell on her. She was there just as regularly, working away in the art room, but she did it now with a total absorption in her work. She only turned to talk if she had something definite to say, not just to chatter. Raju thought she was getting worried about her exams, and it confirmed for him the maturity that made her different from the others.

He had to move fast to stop this new silence from solidifying, from becoming an accepted treaty of distance between them. After all, he'd made his confession and if there was going to be any embarrassment, he had been through it. He thought he should ask her outright, just as the white boys would. The first time would be the only difficult time. He was sure she wouldn't expect it from him. How could he say to her, 'Doing anything later, Kim? Would you like to meet me round the King's Head for a drink?' They would be the wrong words to come out of him. She would laugh. But so what if she laughed, as long as no one heard her. Or him. And if she said yes, then he could see a new kind of existence beginning for him. He would tell her she could take the portait of herself away from school, as a present. They would go together to all the places she talked about, and they would be together in school in the common room and at work in the art room and she would watch him as he became a struggling but successful painter and when he was earning some money from his first job....

Another pressure bore down on his thoughts. If she did accept, how would he take her out? It would mean getting hold of some money and he could do that easily enough by asking his mum and telling her to keep her mouth shut, but what about the next time? Maybe she'd understand and offer to pay for herself. Or maybe he could get a weekend or evening job like Steve and Lesley did and get a few bob to spend on her. If his father found out, or saw them walking down the street together, he wouldn't approve. They would have to meet secretly and keep themselves from all the prying eyes and gossips of the Indian community.

For days he couldn't muster the courage. There were moments when he felt like swallowing the stone that came to his throat when he thought of it, and asking her outright. Then his opportunity came.

Towards the end of the term, Ravi got the group together and, before the lesson ended, told them that there was an exhibition of Cuban paintings at a gallery in town and that they had better go and see it, because the poster technique was perfect and because he'd like to discuss it with them after. 'Better spend your time sussing it, than getting drugged out of your minds at the King's Head.' The class could never tell if Ravi was serious or half-joking, but they promised to take in the posters in the next week.

When they had gone, Raju continued his work. As he worked he felt the presence of someone else in the room, though he had assumed he was alone, and turning round saw Kim. She was sitting on one of the tall stools, her brow wrinkled, silent and uncertain.

'Still here? I'd thought you'd buzzed off.'

'No,' she said. 'I'm just thinking.'

'You'll get cross eyes if you do it too hard.'

She didn't seem to hear him. 'Are your parents very, kind of prejudiced, Raju?'

The question took him by surprise. 'My father don't like Jamaicans,' Raju said.

'I had an argument with my dad last night,' Kim said, 'about Indians. He's really stupid and he was saying they're all jungle bunnies, not as bad as the coons, but still from villages and that.'

'Some are,' Raju said.

'I was telling him about you and how you were the best artist in the class, and you'd be better than the stuff in the galleries, which is half rubbish and a con anyway.'

Raju felt she was steering the conversation in the direction he had watched for.

'He just said that didn't matter, even cave-men could do drawings. He makes me so mad, and he's so thick, he always argues and he knows he's wrong.'

'Why were you talking about Indians?'

He thought he knew what the answer would be. Surely she was looking in his face in that particular way to see what expectation she had stirred in him.

'I don't care. I couldn't give a monkey's what he says, I'll go out with whichever blokes I choose, black or blue or green with horns and bells on.'

To Raju it felt as though the silence was begging to be shattered. 'Would you go out with me?' he asked, 'I mean to the exhibition. To the posters, the Cuban ones.'

She didn't answer immediately and Raju seemed to hear the question echo like a crashing tray of crockery. He had blundered.

'I've seen it,' she said eventually, 'and I couldn't today anyway. You know I'm really getting into my books and exams. I have to leave this dump.'

It was like being slapped in the face. Or it was like jumping and the parachute not opening. He'd snapped the cord by pulling it too soon.

'I don't much care for posters, really,' he said.

'No, you *must* go.' She sensed she had hurt him. 'It's excellent. It gives you a whole new idea of what art can be used for.'

Raju tried to finish his copying, feeling now as though the air was still foggy with his disappointment. What should he do?

Just then Ravi came in. 'Still here?' he said, cheerily. 'I've got to clear out now because I've got to change and come back to school for the third-year parents.'

'I'm coming out too, I've finished,' Kim said.

Out in the street, Raju couldn't allow himself to think about that moment. He had built himself up, prepared himself for the right moment, and now the moment had failed him. He got home, his head still fixed on the scene, and his mother asked him if he was feeling all right and touched his forehead with the back of her hand. Raju shook it off impatiently. He sat in front of the telly all evening, and he wondered how he'd face her the next day. Kim might tell the others that he'd tried to take her out, but that she'd tactfully refused and given him an excuse because she couldn't bring herself to tell him outright that she didn't fancy him. She probably hadn't even heard of the exhibition. She should have made up some other excuse, told him the truth, that she was afraid her father would see her with a black. That too came as a shock to him. He had thought about whites and blacks and discussed it in class and at home but he had always presumed that he wouldn't ever have a severe problem with being black, not with the kids he'd grown up with, or at least not with some of them.

He went up early to bed and lay awake. He couldn't sleep till the early hours of the morning and, when his alarm rang, he shouted downstairs to his mother that he didn't feel well and he wasn't going to school.

Raju lay on his back through the morning. He thought he'd been cowardly, but he couldn't bear to enter that sixth-form room. He moped around the house and refused to go to school for the two remaining days of that week. He read his texts and his notes at home and told himself that since the mock exams were so close, there'd be hardly anyone from his class going in.

For exam weeks the desks were set out in the hall, and

the school changed completely. The younger kids were moved into the lower school and there was no buzzer for periods and no lessons and people came and went as they had to or chose to. Raju went in and did his exams and avoided seeing Kim or any of the seniors who were all engrossed in their A levels. He wasn't allowed in the art room because the art exams were on, and so Raju never got to see Ravi except once when he was on exam duty during maths, giving out blotting paper and graph books.

After the exams Raju didn't go back to school, as some of the others did, to join in the lounging and card-playing and football and cricket sessions that always followed upper school exams. His studies had put Kim to the back of his mind. He had resolved to himself that he'd never ask a white girl out again. She had led him on, he was sure of that. It was her way of breaking that bond of possession that he felt he had built towards her. She had proved to herself that she could humiliate him. And the portrait of her was still his, she hadn't accepted it, hadn't given him the cue to offer it to her. When he thought of the portrait he felt it was a wound he'd inflicted on himself. He wanted to get hold of that portrait now and destroy it, burn it. But he couldn't. Any theatrical action would only give him away. Suppose she hadn't told anyone. She might really have seen the exhibition and really needed her time for study. Then it would be best to act as though nothing had been said, nothing had happened. He could go back to school and continue to be 'nervous', and continue as he had always done and work in the art room for the rest of the term because she would have gone and probably got herself a summer job.

The day Raju went back to school, Ravi was putting up an exhibition of students' work in the hall. 'Hey, we've been trying to get hold of you,' Ravi said. 'You've been away ... are you OK now? ... and we've had an idea. Head's idea really. We're going to have the usual exhibition for inspectors and parents and bods and pick the best work, pottery and jewellery and even paintings, and offer them for sale, flog 'em and give the artists the money minus something for charity. What do you think? Head thinks it'll give you lot a sense of being at work, and time means money, and all that shit.'

Raju agreed it was a good idea. Ravi asked him to sort out all his work and decide what he wanted to sell. The other sixth formers had already put out their best work to flog. The game did make them feel like professionals and for once they were giving a hand with the arrangement of the exhibits.

In the afternoon, Ravi approached him again. Had he decided? Raju had. He handed Ravi the drawings he'd chosen and two canvases.

'You don't want to flog this?' Ravi said when he came to the portrait of Kim.

'Why not? It might get me some money,' Raju said, and Ravi looked at him, surprised at the unfamiliar, strong tone.

Raju didn't go to the exhibition that evening. He had told Ravi that he didn't know about prices and that, so Ravi should do it. He wanted to go to watch the people react to his painting, but he felt he couldn't. If someone wanted to buy it, and he was actually there, he wouldn't want to part with it. If he stayed away they might get rid of it, and he could forget he'd ever painted it.

'I've got almost twenty quid for you,' Ravi told Raju the next day, 'and the Head asked all the artists to contribute what they wanted to the Children's Fund.'

'I'll give half,' Raju said.

'Now hold on, you don't want to go promising. This isn't a con, you know. We'll get everyone together and discuss this whole charity thing and how much you're all willing to part with and so on. After all, it's your work. I tell you, I asked a couple of friends from the Royal College and they said your paintings were really nice. I'd told them about you.'

Raju didn't ask Ravi who'd bought the paintings.

In the sixth-form room later, as Raju was stirring himself a cup of coffee, the Deputy Head, all miniskirt and efficiency bounced in and said, 'I see Kim liked her portrait enough to put her money on it.'

Raju, while acknowledging her compliment with a smile, felt as though her words had only pulled to the front of his mind what he had known deep down. So she had bought it. It must mean that she had lived with the idea of it too. Some of the money he would get would be hers. He would ask how much it sold for and keep that much and give the rest away. She must want him to know that she'd bought it. She'd take it home and treat it like a twin, and she could say to anyone who asked, that the painter was some Indian bloke in her school, and she thought it was quite a good likeness. She would know different, she would remember him differently, he was sure.

At the start of the holidays Raju began working in his uncle's grocery store. He thought of spending Kim's payment and buying himself some clothes, but changed his mind and bought some books instead, on China and India and on art, that Ravi had recommended. School went out of his mind, and after a few weeks so did Kim.

Then one day his mum called him to the phone and said it was his art teacher.

'Raju, you're a hard man to locate. The Head thought I should let you know. Very sad news. Mr Cole died in hospital yesterday, he had another attack. I'm just phoning round and letting all his pupils know, at least your lot, about the funeral and so on.'

'Yes.' It struck Raju that he had forgotten old Cole, and the news shocked him, but he was also somehow glad that Ravi had called him.

'Do you want to go to the funeral?'

'Yes ... I ... I don't know what to wear.'

'Oh anything, it's not like India. The dead don't care anyway. Will you come over to our place at ten tomorrow then? I could take you in the van, it's at Streatham. And later we can come back and chat if you feel like it. I've been meaning to ask you round for some time, after all you're my star pupil now.'

'I'll come at ten o'clock,' he said and Ravi gave him the address.

The next morning, wearing his school jacket and tie, Raju went to Ravi's flat. He rang the bell and Ravi came down, buttoning his shirt. 'Yeah, come in, I've called Steve and Lesley too and they should be here but as usual they'll be late,' Ravi said, taking the stairs two at a time. 'I'll just have a shave if we're going to a funeral,' he said motioning Raju into a room. 'Kim will make you some tea.'

It was a large room, with a thick carpet and floor

cushions and a single settee. There were rows of books and a stereo set. On the wall, between two paintings of what looked to Raju like terribly distorted, agonised human shapes, was his portrait of Kim.

As Kim herself came round the door to the kitchen, Raju was standing in front of the picture. As soon as he saw her he made an effort to pull himself together and went and sat on the settee.

'Do you like it there? Ravi hung it between two of his own pictures. I kept telling him to bring them to school but he ...' The voice seemed to ramble on, Raju wasn't catching the words. '... so I said it doesn't matter what you say ...' she was saying and Raju turned his face towards her. '... so I thought I'd buy it for him, and then he can have something to remind him of the time when we were all pupils and he put us in touch with....'

'Raju?' she said, or at any rate he thought she said. She was asking him, with a housewifely expression on her face if he'd like some tea.

'Yes, of course I want some tea,' he said.

Ravi came back from his shaving and when Lesley and Steve turned up he said, 'You lads can cram into the back of the van, we'd better go.'

It began to drizzle as they laid Mr Cole to rest. The Head was there and several of the teachers and a few pupils. They nodded as Ravi joined the teachers and Kim stood with the other girls. Raju nodded back solemnly. Raju looked at Kim just once as they stood in silence and saw her looking back, hard, at him. Her eyes were asking him to understand, he thought. It seemed to him that he knew that expression intimately, and he wished he hadn't tried to paint it.